NIPPONIA NIPPON

KAZUSHIGE ABE is one of Japan's pre-eminent contemporary writers. A graduate of the Japanese Institute of the Moving Image in Tokyo, he worked as an assistant director before turning his hand to writing. Since winning the Gunzo New Writers' Prize for his first novel, *Amerika no yoru*, he has been awarded several of Japan's most prestigious literary prizes, including the Sei Ito Award, the Mainichi Culture Award, the Akutagawa Prize and the Tanizaki Prize.

KERIM YASAR teaches modern Japanese literature at the University of Southern California. He is active as a translator in a variety of genres and media, from contemporary novels to pre-modern poetry, and has translated more than a hundred feature films in the Criterion Collection library.

KAZUSHIGE ABE

NIPPONIA NIPPON

Translated from the Japanese by

KERIM YASAR

PUSHKIN PRESS

Pushkin Press
Somerset House, Strand
London WC2R 1LA

Original text © Kazushige Abe / CTB Inc., 2001
English translation rights arranged through CTB Inc.
English translation by Kerim Yasar 2023

Nipponia Nippon was first published as
Nipponia Nippon by Shinchosa in Tokyo, 2001

First published by Pushkin Press in 2023

The publisher would like to thank David Karashima, Michael
Emmerich and Elmer Luke for their editorial work and support

Pushkin Press would like to thank the Yanai Initiative for
Globalizing Japanese Humanities at UCLA and Waseda University
for its support

■■■ YANAI INITIATIVE

1 3 5 7 9 8 6 4 2

ISBN 13: 978-1-78227-853-5

Designed and typeset by Tetragon, London
Printed and bound by Clays Ltd, Elcograf S.p.A.

www.pushkinpress.com

NIPPONIA NIPPON

HARUO TOYA narrowed his options down to three: breed them, free them, or kill them.

Realistically speaking, breeding was off the table. Getting these precious, endangered birds from Sado to Tokyo would be impossible enough, but keeping them in a six-mat room? No way, not birds that size. His parents' home—in the countryside the next prefecture over, not too far away—was a possibility, but just getting the place ready would require a massive effort. How was a frail seventeen-year-old boy who had no money and didn't really know where to begin going to do that? The government was struggling to keep the birds alive, and all he was was a kid with a fantasy about taking care of the birds and taming them. Then, he worried, suppose the birds' whereabouts leaked out, things could turn totally crazy.

So, the options were really down to freeing them or killing them. Which meant whatever he decided would be a final solution, no turning back. He put off deciding, but thought about it round the clock. His imagination played the two scenarios over and over; in his indecision it was his only break from complete inertia.

The first thing, in either scenario, was he'd have to break into the cage. Then the next step—liberate or kill. Either course of action, he realized, he felt just fine about. No unease. In a way, the sense of his achievement would be the same.

By letting the birds go, he could feel proud of himself—a hero, a liberator of weak, captive innocents. On the other hand, by killing them, he would be an agent of chaos, crushing the world's good intentions, and he could revel in the ecstasy of a cold-blooded executioner. These were daydreams, of course, but they felt more real to him than reality. He dwelled constantly on these feelings, and his desire to achieve his goal grew stronger by the day.

Justice and injustice coexisted within him. Neither seemed false, yet neither had the upper hand. It was all in his head, anyway. Was there more justice in killing them or letting them go? He could point himself in either direction at will. He wanted to do both. He saw no contradiction in this.

Maybe I really have a split personality, he wondered. It was a thought that came to him often, now as a matter of habit.

Until one of those personalities asserted itself, he entertained both fantasies. But like a slug inching toward its goal, he was driven, surely but slowly, toward the forest where the crested ibises were kept.

●

Haruo had no idea what the security at the Sado Island Crested Ibis Conservation Center was like. The center itself said little on the matter.

An article in the *Mainichi* newspaper's Interactive Crested Ibis Internet Museum page claimed that "the crested ibises seem more carefully supervised than the pandas at Ueno Zoo," but gave no details. Visitors could peer into the cages of the ibises from a designated observation zone that had three mounted sets of binoculars. The cages and adjacent administration building were bordered by a fence, beyond which visitors were not allowed.

The distance between the fence and the cages seemed to be about fifty meters. For what he wanted to do, he wasn't sure whether that was a long distance or not.

In any case, an online map wasn't going to tell him all he needed to know. Since the security for the pandas at Ueno Zoo was, as stated, light in comparison, he went to the zoo to get at least a point of reference. But obviously the situation at Sado was a different story. He needed to go there and do some reconnaissance on his own. But because he was phobic of airplanes and boats, he had no desire to make the trip there more than once.

Photos and maps of the center on various websites showed the aviaries as freestanding structures, unattached to the administrative offices. Immediately he pictured himself, under cover of night, scaling the fence and stealing into the inner compound, sidestepping any defenses. Then he'd break into the aviaries and do his deed, whichever it was to be.

He'd be like Lupin the Third, moving with speed and grace. And when he opened the doors to the aviary and came face-to-face with the birds, he could imagine how *that alone could change the world*. If that moment alone became known, it would give the country a jolt, sparking both praise and outrage. He'd be a hero! He'd be a villain! He'd have done something bold and unprecedented! His fantasies rolled on.

But what if there were guards at night? What if he bumped into a staff member? Crested ibises were "Special Natural Monuments" in Japan and on the IUCN Red List of Threatened Species, so *of course* there'd be staff on night duty, *of course* there'd be security guards patrolling the place.

Professionals always plan for the worst-case scenario. Haruo had read that somewhere. He was only an amateur, but he had to approach this thing like a pro. Failure was not an option. If he got caught, there would be no second chance. He'd be subjected to disdain and mockery all over again. Those pig-shit scumbags, all dressed up, pissing themselves laughing and sticking it to him, the pathetic son of the soba-maker, a bush-league crackpot.

In other words, the world would keep looking at him the way it always had.

So he needed weapons. But if a guard or staff member saw him, a confrontation was unavoidable. He needed protection. He wasn't a scrapper, not in a fist-to-fist kind of way, which wouldn't be practical in any case under the circumstances. He needed weapons that could neutralize any opponent instantly, keep them out of action for a long time. That was how to plan for a worst-case scenario.

He typed "stun gun" in the search field on his computer: 4,195 results came up. He tried another search, adding the keywords "online shopping," and got 1,543 results. Still too many. He refined the search again, adding "handcuffs" and got 32 results. OK. Of those, Haruo selected an Osaka seller boasting "the world's best selection!" and "unbeatable bargains."

He didn't know if the seller really had "the world's best selection," but there sure was a lot. Haruo had bought stuff online before, but never self-defense goods, so it took time for him to find his way around the site. The store had more than ten different types of stun gun alone, but there were also crossbows and slingshots, an array of knives, nunchaku, and extendable batons, even night-vision scopes. He was amazed that all of this was legal.

He wanted to arm himself to the teeth, but he also had to scrape together the funds from his allowance, so he had to be selective. After studying the descriptions of possible items, he chose four weapons based on ease of use, effectiveness, and how well they complemented each other.

For the purpose of disarming an opponent, he chose a stun baton, which had the highest power and the least risk of being snatched away by said opponent. With a length of 46.7 centimeters and a weight of 500 grams, it was a large model, and at 500,000 volts, it was the most powerful in its advertised class. It could immobilize an opponent for more than forty minutes after just five seconds of contact. It was normally 58,000 yen, but thanks to a "limited-time sale," it was now only 12,000 yen. This was the first item he put in his shopping cart.

Next, pepper spray. There were many types, but Haruo had his budget to consider and so he settled on the cheapest (2,200 yen). The spray was composed of capsicum (3%) and sulfur mustard (3%), in a medium of Freon 134a (94%). It caused violent coughing, non-stop sneezing, and intense pain to the eyes, nose, and throat. It had an effective range of two meters, and its neutralizing power would be even greater when combined with the stun baton.

Then, handcuffs. Haruo wasn't sure how many pairs he'd need, but he guessed that two would be enough. According to the Ministry of the Environment's website, the Sado Island Crested Ibis Conservation Center was staffed by "four people: a veterinarian, a breeder, and two assistants." That meant, probably, that at night there'd be one watchman, two at most, and no more than one staff member on site—for a total of three. Even if there were others, a 500,000-volt stun baton would knock them out instantly. Haruo added two sets of double-lock nickel handcuffs (2,800 yen each) to the cart.

Finally, a knife—or, as stated, a "survival knife"; it'd be a backup weapon if the stun baton failed. A knife was easier to use than something like a crossbow; it was light, yet lethal in close-quarter combat. A stun baton wouldn't kill, but a blade could neutralize an opponent for good. It would also be useful if he decided his "final solution" was to kill the birds. The selection of knives was quite large. From the offerings Haruo chose a 30-centimeter knife with a 17.5-centimeter blade for the price of 7,000 yen. It came in a leather sheath and with several accessories: matches, a compass, a grindstone, fishing lines, hooks, and weights. He'd have no use for it after his mission, so a cheap one would do. He added it to his cart.

With consumption tax and a 1,000-yen fee for cash on delivery, his total came out to 29,140 yen (shipping was free on orders over 20,000 yen). Haruo's budget was 30,000 yen, so he was pleased with his purchase.

He reviewed his strategy: the gear he'd acquired would be enough to neutralize any men he encountered. After all, the guards wouldn't be carrying more than a nightstick, and it was unlikely that the center was on alert for a terrorist attack. Nonetheless, if the police were called, these weapons wouldn't be enough: policemen carry guns. A stun baton or a survival knife was no match for that. Slingshots and crossbows were projectile weapons, but couldn't be fired rapidly or continuously, and couldn't be mastered in the short time that he had. For a mission like this, he really needed parity with his opponent. If he wanted to be certain of success, he needed a gun. This was going to cost him, but like a pro, he was preparing for the worst-case scenario.

Where to get a gun? In the movies, in novels, people got them from the yakuza, but Haruo wanted to steer clear of such sinister types. He turned again to the internet.

Following links from a list of Dark Web websites, he landed on The Inside Dope, which turned out to be a valuable resource for all kinds of illicit activity. He posted an anonymous message on the forum: "I'm looking for a real gun." He provided a free email address and said he could pay up to 150,000 yen. That was one month of his allowance, meant to cover rent and living expenses.

According to a survey carried out in autumn 1998 by the National Federation of University Co-operative

Associations (NFUCA), university students living in apartments in Tokyo received an average monthly allowance of 111,830 yen. Haruo wasn't going to school, nor did he have a part-time job, let alone full-time employment. Nonetheless, every month he received from his parents an allowance considerably higher than the average, and was able to do with it as he pleased.

And so he was free to spend his days surfing the internet and contemplating the plight of the crested ibises. Holed up in his apartment, undisturbed by anyone, he had been at it for three months, since October 2000. Somewhere in that time he had had a job, but it didn't last two weeks. He wasn't a complete recluse, a real *hikikomori*, nor was he obsessed with the ibises 24/7, but as one month led to the next and then the next, the ibises became the main focus of his attention.

At the end of January 2001, Haruo had settled on "the final solution" to "the *Nipponia nippon* problem." It became clear to him when he learned that the plumage of the birds Yu Yu and Mei Mei had changed, signaling the onset of the breeding season.

Two days after Haruo placed his weapons order, it arrived.

He handed over 29,140 yen to the courier, stamped his seal on the delivery receipt, and took possession of the goods. It all seemed so easy. The seller's website had read, "We are not permitted to sell self-defense products to minors," but Haruo was never asked his age, nor to provide identification. Just like that, he was halfway there.

The gun was another matter. Soon after he posted his message on the forum, he received three email messages that treated him like a child: "150,000 yen? Are you out of your mind? If you're that poor, just stick to air guns," "Don't you know the Juvenile Law is even harsher on weapon possession than before? Stop pretending to be an adult, punk!" and "If you want a gun, join the Self-Defense Forces."

He got no other responses. Chided, Haruo went on the forum again, raising his offer to 300,000 yen. Within six hours, he received an email with the subject line "I'm selling a Tokarev (8 rounds included)." The sender claimed that the gun was "authentic" and had been test-fired. Haruo was pleased but hesitant, since the deal was dependent on the seller receiving the entire 300,000 yen before the weapon would be sent.

The internet was rife with scams, and demanding payment up front without delivering the goods was a common one. How could Haruo trust this guy? He had no way of knowing if the seller was on the level, and he had no confidence in his ability to negotiate a better deal. Seeing how this was all illegal anyway, he certainly couldn't run to the authorities if he got ripped off. Stuck, he decided to do nothing—and see if the seller contacted him again. That was the only way to determine the seller's true intentions.

●

Haruo was in his first year of middle school when he discovered, flipping through a dictionary, that *to*, the first kanji of his surname, could also be read as *toki*, the meaning of which was "crested ibis."

This was a major moment, and it made him feel an affinity for the bird. It began modestly, with the crested ibis becoming his favorite species. He didn't bother to read up on them, but when crested ibises were ever in the news, he found himself paying attention.

What fascinated him more than the birds themselves was their predicament. They were extremely rare—endangered, in fact—and they were bred under a national conservation and breeding program. All this made Haruo feel that he, too, was special. That his surname, Toya ("crested ibis valley"), shared the same kanji with the *toki* not only confirmed this, it was a sign of nobility, he believed. It was alienating that nobody could understand why he was so proud of his name, but this only strengthened his sense of grandeur.

Haruo didn't know when to shut up. He was constantly trying to get his classmates to acknowledge his superior intellect and unique ideas. Unsurprisingly, they avoided him, kept him at a distance. His logorrhea spilled over into his writing as well: every day, at home, he filled the pages of his diary with outpourings of emotion, while at school he would talk his classmates' ears off. His long-windedness and attention-seeking were an irritation. He could tell that he rubbed people the wrong way, but he lacked the self-control to do anything about it.

His grades were good, not great, and he had an average build, but he could be ferocious in a fight, so he didn't get beaten up very often. Instead, there was a period when his stuff got hidden or ripped up. He knew who his tormentors were, so he responded in kind. This deterred them a bit, and after a particularly nasty period things did calm down. The bullying ended when he entered his third year and was moved to another homeroom. The bullies had by then turned their attention to another outcast.

In his three years of middle school, Haruo didn't make a single close friend; it felt to him that he had spent the entire time delivering monologues. Yet it never occurred to him to alter his image simply by talking less, and he refused to play the game of self-deprecation that lubricated social interactions. Like many his age, he was impatient with the world without understanding it. He believed that when he became an adult, he would find an environment where he felt he belonged. His ideal was a world without enmity or malice, a tender world of kindness and respect, a paradise where crested ibises flew freely in the sky.

His awareness of the birds' predicament, and his sympathy toward them, grew over time.

The January before Haruo entered high school, China gifted Japan with two crested ibises, Yang Yang and Yo Yo, who were in residence at the Sado Island Crested Ibis Conservation Center. In May, the birth of a crested ibis chick through artificial breeding—the first such case in Japan—became big news. Haruo felt as if this all had been his personal good fortune, but he said nothing because he hated the idea of joining the herd that was fixated on the news. The day the chick was born, he wrote in his diary: "I can't express my feelings, because then I'd be like everyone else." Although the media treated the conservation and breeding program as a project of national interest, Haruo saw it as a passing fad. When he learned that the name of the chick would be selected from a pool of suggestions submitted by elementary school students, he was disgusted: here was a sublime creature, on the verge of extinction, being treated like a carnival sideshow. It made him furious. Whatever pleasure he felt dissipated each time news about the chick came on TV.

Something was fundamentally wrong about this whole thing. A vague sense of the wrong grew more clear to him each day, and as he committed the sense of this wrong to his diary, he nailed it: people thought that the birth of the chick, named Yu Yu, had saved *Nipponia nippon,* the Japanese crested ibis, from extinction, when the fact of the matter was Yu Yu may have been born on Japanese soil but was the offspring of crested ibises from China. The extinction of the indigenous bird was a foregone conclusion!

Once he realized this, all of the festivities over "the second-generation crested ibis" seemed like a sham. People just wanted an excuse to cheer about something, anything. The gloom of "the endless recession" no doubt had something to do with it. As usual, people wanted to turn away from reality and forget their troubles. They were making merry, nothing more. It may be a cliché to say this, but feeling scorn for "the masses" from a position of no responsibility is easy.

Haruo studied the press coverage, trying to get to the heart of the matter. He came to the following conclusion: this national fixation on the birds' breeding amounted to no more than a vulgar interest in the sex life of the ibises. *That* was the kind of society he lived in. It was true that Japanese think about nothing but sex. And not just human sex: there were probably people masturbating to the mating of birds.

First, they kill off all the ibises, mercilessly, and now they breed a single bird, artificially, and they think they've saved the species. But imagining the birds *actually having sex*—that was the extra thrill!

I don't want anything to do with this animal abuse, Haruo declared to himself. At the least, he would stop obsessing over the birds. He would not be swept up by the herd. But it didn't mean he'd be able to stop caring about the birds altogether.

After Haruo arrived in Tokyo on the first day of October the previous year, he was tormented by a deep loneliness, which drew him back into the world of the ibises. He hadn't had many friends to begin with, and in the city he didn't know anyone, so his days passed with him unable even to strike up a conversation. He also had to bear the pain of not being able to gaze upon the face of the girl he loved. During those days of solitude, as he searched for something, anything, that could give him an emotional anchor, he recalled how the first kanji in his surname translated into "crested ibis" and it was this fact that provided him a clue to his salvation. But this renewed sense of identification with the ibises was different than before.

Haruo's life had changed radically that autumn. He dropped out of high school and moved from his hometown to Tokyo, beginning a life on his own. This hadn't been his idea; it was his parents', which he'd agreed to. At first he was angry, thinking they were unfair, but he had come to believe that it was the right decision. The fact that he couldn't tell his beloved how much he loved her, the fact that he quit school, the fact that he had to leave his hometown—all of this was his fate. The world where everybody loved and respected everybody else did not exist.

In the past, he had numbed himself to his loneliness by escaping into a world of fantasy. It was his only recourse, young and inexperienced as he was. When he first arrived in Tokyo, he groped around for some way to break through the city's unjust barriers and, indeed, for a reason to be alive at all. This threw him into a depression.

Now a path emerged clearly before his eyes. It had taken a while, but now he had a purpose in life. His fantasies were no longer a way of escaping reality; rather, they were training for a goal. *No matter how great the sacrifice, I must succeed.* It was an epiphany. For better or worse, the plight of the crested ibises had got him to this moment.

The computer was his most valuable resource in learning about the birds. When he agreed to leave home, Haruo conditioned it upon his parents' paying for a new laptop and a high-speed internet connection. If he was being exiled to a strange place, he was entitled to it. If he could surf the web to his heart's content, he could endure any hardship in Tokyo. It gave him *something* to look forward to. At home with his parents there was only a dial-up connection and a computer he was forced to share with his younger brother. In Tokyo he would at least be able to use the computer as much as he pleased.

Shiro Misawa, his father's old high school classmate, helped him settle in Tokyo. He took charge of everything from finding Haruo an apartment to finding him a job. His wife purchased all the necessary household items. On moving day, Haruo had only to go buy a laptop and a mobile phone with his parents; the Misawas had taken care of everything else. Before nightfall, his apartment was in order and the internet connection was up and running. The following day, Misawa took Haruo and his parents to the Western-style pastry shop he owned and offered Haruo a job.

"I'm going to turn Shunsaku the soba-maker's son into a first-rate pastry chef!" Misawa said, laughing loudly.

Haruo got the strong impression that this was done more out of ostentation than of friendship. He gave Misawa and his parents sidelong glances as they chatted, disdainful of their insincere smiles. That said, it didn't bother him to be working there. He had no desire to become a pastry chef, but he didn't mind having a job to go to.

He worked in the pastry shop by day, then surfed the web almost until the break of dawn. After a week of this, the lack of sleep made it harder for him to go to work, and he started showing up late. He knew that he had the so-called "internet addiction," but he couldn't stop. Even when he was doing chores at work, he got restless, thinking about things he'd read on online forums the night before. He was getting fed up with the job, and it became more and more difficult just to leave the house. At home, he would often plunge into depression or be rocked by violent impulses, but even that seemed better than going to his job. Surfing the web was much more educational than learning how to make pastries; for him, it was indispensable.

In the past, his idle thoughts and lukewarm interests would quickly fade and be forgotten, but now he scoured the web to understand everything that caught his attention. Learning about things online eased his loneliness. He had passed his first days in Tokyo not doing much, but everything changed once he had found his purpose in life.

With nobody to talk to, he poured out his thoughts and feelings endlessly in his diary, and since the computer was limited only by its disk space, he didn't have to hold back. On screen, his writing seemed cogently argued and crystal-clear. He never doubted that he was on the right path. Everything that had happened to him up to that point finally seemed to fit together. His life had direction and meaning. It was only his baseless fears that told him otherwise.

His surname was a major impulse in his surfing online. His first search left him disappointed. He had wanted to confirm that "Toya" was a rare and enviable name, only to discover it was hardly rare at all. He got relatively few hits for "Toya" (49), and that was gratifying, but he was surprised to learn how many other surnames contained the kanji for "crested ibis" in them. So many, in fact, that Haruo felt mortified at having bragged about it in middle school. There was Tokita, Tokizawa, Tonosu, Tokinami, Tokine, and even Toki, written with that one same kanji. And those were just the ones he had found. Toya was only one among others, and the name started to seem ordinary, even insipid.

He did a search to see which name using that kanji was the rarest of all; this left him even more dejected. In descending order, he found 1,640 hits for Tokita, 157 for Tokizawa, 69 for Tonosu, 30 for Tokinami, and 2 for Tokine (he didn't bother with Toki because it was impossible to isolate the surnames from all the other hits that popped up). Toya was in the middle, with 49 hits, which did nothing to change his feeling of its unremarkability.

Though he was disappointed, the keyword "toki" did yield for him some interesting information: there was a place called Toya in Nagara-machi, Chosei County, Chiba Prefecture, and there were other places in Chiba that had the same character for crested ibis in their name. Apparently, the prefecture had once been a breeding grounds for crested ibises.

NTT East Japan's Hello Net Japan website, which featured local information produced by regional offices, had this to say about the city of Togane in Chiba:

Toward the end of the Muromachi Period, the Chiba clan built Tokigamine Castle (Crested Ibis Peak Castle) in the village of Hetakata, which now corresponds to the area surrounding Lake Hakkaku. It was named Tokigamine because of the many crested ibises gathered there at the time. Some people speculate that "Tokigamine" was later changed into "Togane."

Of course, Haruo was moved to believe that his ancestors had lived in Chiba, probably even in the town of Toya itself. They had surely seen flocks of crested ibises in flight, then watched as the magnificent birds plunged from the sky to feed on loaches, river crabs, mud snails. They must surely have witnessed people lying in wait, capturing the birds alive or stoning them dead, plucking their feathers, eating their flesh. People who came in hordes and slaughtered the birds without restraint, pushing them to the brink of extinction. But—

Could one of my ancestors have done those awful deeds? What if my family lived in Toya and made a living hunting the birds? Is that the root of my obsession?

Haruo knew he'd never learn the answer to those questions, and he wasn't going to try. His parents had severed ties with the main branch of the Toya family long ago. They had retained the family name, but there was no supposed head of the family and nobody in town shared the name. His grandfather Mamoru Toya had left home on September 19, 1988, and never returned, but Haruo's parents had been estranged from that side of the family long before that. Miyo, Haruo's grandmother, had forbidden the family from ever mentioning Mamoru's name, and even when her grandchildren asked about him, she refused to respond. Mamoru had left home without a word, and Miyo wanted to forget he ever existed.

Haruo was five when his grandfather disappeared. His parents never fully explained what happened, but he guessed that Mamoru had run off with another woman. He didn't pursue it further, since his knowing wouldn't change anything and certainly wouldn't benefit him. He had no sympathy for his grandfather, and no desire to meet him. His memories of him were faint and included no lost affection. Mamoru felt like a distant relative.

Whatever the truth of his ancestors might have been, Haruo proceeded with his fantasies unchecked. So what if he had ibis-hunting ancestors. He wasn't interested in actual history. What mattered was his own inescapable lot in life.

Maybe the family name Toya isn't a sign of nobility, after all; maybe I've been branded as part of the bloodline of killers of the crested ibis. The thought brought up wretched and repugnant images that gave him the chills, yet his imagination could not be reined in. He grew only more agitated. Haunted by visions of a blood-soaked past, he put his hand on his crotch to calm himself down. He wished he had someone to talk to, but there was no one. He was alone. An endless stream of unutterable words swirled around in his head.

With this revived interest in the ibises came a dreamy nostalgia—a nostalgia into which he sought to escape completely. *How are the crested ibises in Sado doing?*

On the morning of Sunday, October 15, television news reported that Mei Mei, the female crested ibis sent from China as a gift upon Premier Zhu Rongji's visit to Japan, had arrived at the Sado Island Crested Ibis Conservation Center in Niibo Village, Niigata Prefecture.

Misawa's pastry shop was closed on the first and third Sunday of every month, so Haruo had been up all Saturday night, surfing the web. He was about to shut down the computer and go to bed when the news caught his attention. Upon hearing the words that Mei Mei had been selected "to mate with Yu Yu," Haruo's heart began to race.

This was a sign! Mei Mei's arrival in Japan wasn't just a turn of events, it was an auspice—and certainly *not* a coincidence that it should happen exactly as his interest in the crested ibises had been rekindled.

It was then, in a moment that felt enchanted by the birds, that the word "destiny" first floated to the surface of his consciousness. "Destiny..." It sounded so pretentious when he said it aloud. And ominous. He felt unease; but worse: It was terror.

More, he thought. *I have to learn more about the crested ibises.*

He never returned to work at the pastry shop.

●

Per the Japanese search engine Goo's "Handy Japanese Dictionary Tool":

From the *Daijirin* Japanese Dictionary, courtesy of Sanseido:

toki (n.) 【鴇・〈朱鷺〉・〈桃花鳥〉】

A bird in the Threskiornithidae family within the Pelecaniformes order. Scientific name *Nipponia nippon.* Total length is approximately 75 centimeters. The entire body is covered with white plume, with long crown feathers on the back of the head. The wings and tail feathers are salmon pink (also known as "crested-ibis color" in Japanese) while the legs and unfeathered parts of the face are red. During the breeding season the feathers turn gray. The beak is black and long with a downward curve. The wild species became extinct in Japan in 1981 and the birds are only bred in Shaanxi Province, China. It has been designated a Special Natural Monument and is on the IUCN Red List of Threatened Species.

According to the *Shinsen Jikyo* Chinese–Japanese dictionary, *tsuki* is another way to read the kanji 鴇 and functions as another word for the crested ibis. It was clear, in any case, that the kanji has no meaning other than "crested ibis." With that confirmation, Haruo proceeded with his research on the birds.

But when he found that there were more than nine thousand web pages about crested ibises, he knew he had to narrow his focus. Haruo first looked at the public websites of the Sado Island Crested Ibis Conservation Center and the Environmental Agency (which on January 6, 2001 would be renamed the Ministry of the Environment) then read through a few newspaper articles. That alone took days, but it didn't feel like work. He was so engrossed that he read with a degree of concentration that was new for him.

As he began to understand the workings of the protection and breeding programs, he grew even more disturbed by the public excitement that had greeted Yu Yu's birth. Efforts had been at cross-purposes with one another and critical details had been obscured.

He wrote the following in his diary:

> The crested ibises are being kept isolated in a facility surrounded by many trees. The state takes good care of the birds and keeps them alive, but every day, large numbers of tourists come to gawk at them. The state's main concern is that the ibises mate and reproduce, and everyone hopes that, even if it happens only once, many chicks will be born. The last thing anybody wants is for the *Nipponia nippon* lineage to be broken.

But, Haruo reasoned, the extinction of the native Japanese crested ibis was already a given: the last male

Japanese ibis, Midori, died suddenly on April 30, 1995, and all of the eggs laid by Fan Fan, who had been borrowed from China to mate with Midori, had not been fertilized. The only remaining Japanese crested ibis was Kin, who was old and no longer able to reproduce.

Haruo opened the administrative resource page on the website of the Natural Environment Office of the Environmental Agency and found the following:

THE STATE OF THE CRESTED IBIS IN JAPAN AND CHINA
Survival only in Japan and China—taxonomically identical
Scientific name: *Nipponia nippon*

As of the end of 1998, one bird in Japan, more than 130 birds in China

Specimen in Japan: "Kin," female, 31 years old; no longer able to breed

In residence at the Sado Island Japanese Crested Ibis Conservation Center as part of the Environmental Agency's protected breeding effort

SPECIMENS IN CHINA

1981 Rediscovered in the Qinling Mountains in Shaanxi Province
1983 Crested Ibis Natural Reserve established in Yangxian County, Shaanxi Province
1998 Number of wild birds increased to 60, number in captivity increased to 71

CHINA–JAPAN COOPERATION

1. BREEDING

Loan of Hoa Hoa from China to Japan, 1985–1989 (four breeding seasons): Hoa Hoa (male) was lent by the Beijing Zoo to be mated with Kin (female) at Sado; returned to China without success.

Loan of Midori from Japan to China, 1990–1992 (three breeding seasons): Midori (male) was lent by Sado to be paired with Yao Yao (female) at the Beijing Zoo; returned to Japan without success.

Loan of a pair from China to Japan, 1994–1995 (one breeding season): Long Long (male) and Feng Feng (female) was lent by the Crested Ibis Natural Reserve in Yangxian Country to reproduce at Sado; Feng Feng returned to China after sudden death of Long Long.

2. COOPERATION WITH CHINESE PRESERVATION EFFORTS

To date, thanks to the Japan International Cooperation Agency, the Environmental Agency, private foundations, fundraising efforts, etc.:

- Provision of breeding facilities and equipment such as surveillance cameras and vehicles
- Dispatch of researchers and breeding experts
- Support for habitat surveys
- Support for public awareness projects
- Other forms of support

Since this information was current only as of late 1998, it did not include Yu Yu, who was born the following year, nor Shin Shin and Ai Ai, who were born even later. Haruo wondered how they would figure into the diagram of the relationship between Japan and China. It seemed to him that, as part of a Chinese lineage born in Japan, they would muddy the waters.

Yu Yu, Shin Shin, Ai Ai—how would the Japanese public regard this new generation of ibises and their ambiguous identities? Haruo looked at this next:

One-Page Crested Ibis Special Edition: What's Your Nationality?
Yu Yu's Soliloquy

June 17, 2000 Kyodo News A3T637 Society 308S02 (537 characters)

My name is Yu Yu. A year after I was born on Sado Island in Niigata, my sibling came into the world. But there's something that bothers me: even though we were born in Japan, aren't we actually "Chinese birds"? The people around us have all sorts of different ideas about this.

"Should we make a family register for the chick? Does the principle of territorial privilege apply here, or that of personal privilege?" When I was born in May of last year, this was apparently what the late Keizo Obuchi, prime minister at the time, had asked. An official in the Wildlife Division of the Environmental Agency said, "Since our agency is responsible for the bird, its nationality is Japanese." But things were more complicated: "Since the bird originated in China… it may be more accurate to say that it has no Japanese nationality."

Shoji Shinozuka, professor emeritus of civil law at Waseda University, argued that I was Japanese. "Since the bird was given as a gift to the Emperor, we may consider it his personal property, which he has entrusted to the care of the Environmental Agency."

Okimasa Murakami, an assistant professor of wildlife biology at the Kyoto University Graduate School of Science, commented: "This bird may have different ancestors from the Japanese crested ibis. A genetic analysis should have been carried out to determine if they are in fact of the same species. But since the bird has arrived on Japanese soil, it may be thought to have acquired Japanese nationality."

Michihiro Osawa, lawyer and Niigata City ombudsman, said: "Under the present circumstances, I don't think that our residents can be persuaded to use tax money to finance the breeding of this bird. We need their consent to designate the ibis as Japanese."

None of this relieves my anxieties, so all I can do is learn from my grandma Kin and try hard to increase the number of Japanese crested ibises.

Haruo found all of this incredibly disingenuous (aka such bullshit). His annotation:

If the focus is supposed to be on preservation and breeding, all of this stuff about nationality is pointless. It's as if the fact that the bird's scientific name is Nipponia nippon means that the question is permanently tied to the fate of the nation. In other words, isn't it precisely because of the name Nipponia nippon that its preservation and breeding is considered so important and gets so much attention? I feel that the Japanese crested ibis gets preferential treatment compared to other species that are in danger of extinction.

People in this country keep insisting that Yu Yu and others, as members of the species Nipponia nippon, are Japanese birds, but they aren't actually sure. I have no idea who profits from this or how, but there are more than a few people who are more obsessed with the name Nipponia nippon than with the living creatures themselves. It's almost like they think that the birds' fate will affect the country's fate.

But even though the crested ibis gets preferential treatment, it never goes beyond what's convenient for their human caretakers. Yu Yu and others in the new generation are mere playthings. That, or they're kept alive simply so that the Japanese crested ibis can be revived and the scientific name *Nipponia nippon* can endure.

The more information Haruo collected, the deeper those doubts grew.

On the "Special Features" page of Niigata-Asahi.com, he found the article "Crested Ibis Diary," dated November 19, 2000, which read:

Professor Susumu Ishii (biologist) of Waseda University has announced that DNA analysis of Chinese and Japanese crested ibises has shown that the two are genetically relatively close… Professor Ishii says, "This supports the idea that they are not just taxonomically, but also genetically, the same species." He adds that, in the future, there will be ways to pair birds on the basis of genetics instead of just age and affinity.

Haruo didn't know what to make of "genetically relatively close." He took it to mean that the birds are not exactly the same.

He entered the keywords "Susumu Ishii Waseda crested ibis genes" and ran a search. Nine results appeared, and Haruo proceeded to the Waseda University publicity site, "Waseda Weekly," which had more information. Under "Research Frontlines," which featured the research of Waseda faculty members, Installment 919 (November 20, 2000), was devoted to the work of Professor Susumu Ishii of the School of Education: "Save the Crested Ibis from Extinction! Genetic Research Goes Face-to-Face with the Secret of Life—The Waseda Network that

Connects the University to Sado." Professor Ishii is quoted as follows:

> Inbreeding between close relatives, such as between parents and children or between siblings, is not a very good idea. On the other hand, if the mating partners are too genetically dissimilar, they are no longer the same species, and the continued existence of the Japanese crested ibis is thrown into doubt. Our current investigation shows that the level of genetic similarity is just right. A good analogy might be the difference between Japanese and Chinese people.

So, basically, Yu Yu, Shin Shin, and Ai Ai are not *Japanese*, they are *Chinese*. To use Professor Ishii's own words, they are "not just taxonomically, but also genetically" Chinese crested ibises. This, in itself, was not that important. What really caught Haruo's attention was the following line:

> A Chinese crested ibis might be able to lay an egg with the genes of a Japanese crested ibis.

Ironically, Installment 919 of "Research Frontlines" in "Waseda Weekly" was written on the movement to revive the Japanese crested ibis using cloning technology. Cells had been taken from Midori's vital organs and cryopreserved, and there was likelihood that they would be used for cloning attempts in the future. The Environmental Agency was in fact promoting such a plan, called the "Crested Ibis Preservation and Restoration Project," upon Professor Ishii's recommendation.

Haruo thought was that this was dangerous. Dangerous for whom? For the ibises. The "Crested Ibis Preservation and Recovery Project" would absolutely make the lives of Yu Yu and Shin Shin and Ai Ai more precarious.

Haruo put his opinion down in writing:

The people involved in the Crested Ibis Preservation and Restoration Project won't be happy until they've recovered the Japanese crested ibis by any possible means. They're obsessed with maintaining the Japanese bloodlines… It's just like the issue of "citizenship." In other words, while they go around making noise about how their mission is to preserve and propagate the rare crested ibis, in reality their most important goal is to "preserve" and "propagate" and "conserve" and "restore" the name and blood and nation of *Nippon*. That is, Japan.

This is a reasonable doctrine for the organs of the state. One could say it's utterly predictable. The only thing that matters to the nation is the framework of the nation, so in that sense they're not wrong. There's no need for them to feel ashamed at mercilessly destroying the environment on the one hand, while mouthing slogans about the need to preserve and revive endangered species on the other. For the nation, the mere fact that a creature like the crested ibis is multiplying doesn't mean anything.

In that case, what will become of Yu Yu, Shin Shin, and Ai Ai? Aren't they being kept alive only so that the effort to start cloning the Japanese crested ibis can get off the ground? Professor Ishii's words that "a Chinese crested ibis might be able to lay an egg with the genes of a Japanese crested ibis" seemed to support this. Since Yu Yu, Shin Shin, and Ai Ai were "Chinese crested ibises," didn't that mean they were simply thought of as surrogates to lay eggs "with the genes of a Japanese crested ibis"? And if this was the case, what would happen to Yu Yu, Shin Shin, and Ai Ai once they gave birth to chicks cloned from Japanese ibises such as Midori? Was there any guarantee that second-generation Chinese ibises born in Japan wouldn't be subjected to genetic discrimination?

Haruo stopped typing. He felt that he had to do something to help the ibises, especially Yu Yu, Shin Shin, and Ai Ai. But he felt driven less by righteous indignation than by the sense that he had drawn a winning lottery number. He felt as if one half of his destiny had come into view.

Most of Haruo's questions were addressed in an article from the morning edition of the *Mainichi Shinbun,* June 17, 1999. "Through a Reporter's Eyes: Good News About the Crested Ibis—Excessive Excitement Greets a Domestic First," by Yasuhiro Suzuki of the Niigata bureau:

There's also the sense that too much has been made of this. For whom is the breeding being carried out? Will the chick born to parents brought from China receive Japanese citizenship? The "good news" stories keep coming, but without any answers to these and other questions.

Many in the media, myself included, heralded this "first time for Japan," even while pointing out that the parent birds were from China. Then there were those who, from the beginning, maintained that the birds were Chinese. These positions seem mutually incompatible on the surface, but I think that they both, in fact, subconsciously embrace a kind of nationalism.

There were those who, upon the chick's birth, gleefully proclaimed it a triumph of "crested ibis diplomacy." The local business community, suffering from decreasing tourism, decided that this was an opportunity not to be missed. The issue of breeding the ibises, which had been an "environmental question," suddenly became "a diplomatic question" and "an economic question." I can't help but feel that all of this is proceeding according to script, a script written by human beings.

Right on! Haruo thought this Suzuki guy was completely correct. But having a sound argument by itself was not enough, it was not going to solve the problem. *I'm going to rip this "script written by human beings" into pieces*, Haruo decided, *that's what I'm going to do*—and it felt good. For the first time in a long time, he had made a decision that filled him with excitement.

It never occurred to Haruo that he might be one of those people using the ibises to feel good about himself. He didn't doubt his own good intentions. Ultimately, though, the ibises were a means to justify his end—the destruction of the "script written by human beings." It would be some time before he understood this.

For the moment, the excitement of finding a radical ambition in life overshadowed all of his darker emotions. The mere thought of how he would rip that human script into pieces thrilled him. Lurking within that thrill was the dream of the shock and despair his actions would leave behind, of the deepest emotions he would agitate. And of the hope that he would no longer be kept apart from Sakura Motoki.

●

Haruo blamed Shiro Misawa as the reason that he wasn't going to work. Misawa not only worked him like a slave, but behaved violently toward him. Haruo told his parents there was no way he would work for such a man. He also said he was viciously bullied by the other employees. All of these were lies.

Misawa never hit him. And while the mood in the shop wasn't especially pleasant, the working environment wasn't remotely harsh. It was a well-known and well-liked establishment in the neighborhood, and had even once been featured in a magazine. For his part, Misawa felt he was being obliging with Haruo, whom he saw as a troubled young man living alone for the first time under difficult circumstances. Misawa had dealt with troubled young people before and Haruo didn't appear to be the defiant delinquent type, so Misawa felt confident that he could handle him. As they worked together, Misawa even began to feel he could rely on Haruo. What a miscalculation.

On the morning of his third missed day of work, Haruo was roused by insistent knocking on his door. It was Misawa. On the first missed day Misawa had called Haruo, who claimed to have a cold. On the second day, Misawa's wife had brought food and medicine for him, and discovered that he wasn't actually sick. When

Misawa knocked on his door on the third day, Haruo
wouldn't let him in. Misawa had a spare key, but the
door was secured by a latch chain. He tried to force the
door open by pressing his body into the gap. Haruo lit a
lighter and held it up to Misawa's face and hands, which
caused Misawa to let out a yelp and jump back. His true
colors came out: he screamed at Haruo, threatening to
turn him over to the police. Then, catching his breath,
he calmed down and started speaking in a reasonable
monotone, lecturing Haruo, who ignored him. After
about an hour of this, Misawa gave up and left.

Three days later, on a Saturday, Haruo's parents came
to Tokyo from the countryside, but Haruo wouldn't let
them in to his apartment either. Doing their best not to
provoke him, they pleaded gently. No matter what his
reasons, they promised not to force him to go back to
work, but wouldn't he please just talk with them. His
mother sniffled as she said they couldn't return home
without seeing him, while his father said nothing but
from time to time pounded on the door.

Haruo looked out the peephole. What he saw was a
middle-aged couple so pathetic and despondent that
they might as well have been at a funeral. He stared at
this idiotic scene for several seconds, feeling as if he
was watching a bad movie. This was the first time he

had viewed them through a lens, but this scene was nothing new: his parents' heads had been bowed since June. Thanks to their son's misdeeds, they had had to bow and scrape and apologize to the high school, to the police, and to the Motoki family. Haruo figured that parenthood wasn't easy, but he still had no sympathy for them. He thought that parents who did nothing but apologize were shallow. He even asked his father, who had been a Self-Defense Forces officer, why he couldn't just beat the shit out of anyone who dared to complain.

Shunsaku, Haruo's father, had belonged to the 20th Infantry Regiment of the Ground Self-Defense Forces. Six years after he married into the family, his father-in-law Mamoru disappeared; this prompted Shunsaku to leave the SDF the following year and go back to run the family's soba shop. Now over forty, he looked painfully emaciated for a man who had spent over ten years training for combat; he had turned into a mild-mannered pacifist. He'd been a carouser in his day, but after changing professions he settled down and earned a reputation in the neighborhood as the serious and responsible proprietor of the soba shop.

Haruo despised his father. After finishing middle school, he openly mocked him. He hated the family business, and thought his father's leaving the SDF was a shameful capitulation. Shunsaku could only turn a blind eye toward his son's impudence, and grew increasingly silent even in his own home.

Haruo finally let his mother into the apartment, but her alone. His father decided to return to the pastry shop to apologize again to Misawa. Haruo said nothing as he stared at his retreating father's back with contempt.

His mother entered the apartment and sat down on the tatami floor in the formal *seiza* posture. From his position on his bed, Haruo looked down at his mother and told his side of the story. He didn't waste the opportunity: it was the first time in a long time that anybody was bothering to listen to him patiently, he said. He jumped from one wild claim to another, making Misawa out to be the villain. His mother, Mizue, nodded sympathetically, pretending to believe his lies. At one point she interrupted him, asking if she should call the police since things were that bad. He muttered that that wouldn't be necessary. She nodded, then continued softly, as if speaking to a small child, "Then what will you do, Haru-chan? Will you look for another part-time job?"

He said nothing for a while. He had just begun researching the crested ibis and hadn't decided upon his objective on that front. He was idle much of the time. What he really wanted to do was to return home and see Sakura Motoki, the object of his true affection, but he knew that if he took one step toward her, her parents would have the police arrest him. He'd have to be prepared before he tried such a thing. It wasn't the right time, and besides, he wanted to forget about her, if possible. She was going to reduce him to a monkey who could do nothing but rub his dick all day, and who would eventually be thrown into a cage in the zoo, robbed of his wits and willpower. Or that was the catastrophe he imagined in order to repress his yearning. He knew that as long as he was infatuated with her, his thoughts would go around in circles and his life would go nowhere. But he was still young, and it wasn't that easy for him to control his feelings. He kept pining for her even after moving to Tokyo, and his deep solitude only fueled his inner conflicts.

"What will you do?" his mother asked again.

He'd rather study than work, was what he came up with. He would take the high-school equivalency exam the next year and, if he passed, take the university entrance exam after that. His mother's face brightened into a smile, and she placed her palms together as if in grateful prayer. She seemed genuinely happy.

Mizue's ability to see through Haruo's lies should have sharpened in the last six months, but upon hearing him say something positive and ambitious, she allowed her maternal love to erase all doubt. When he added that he'd arrived at this decision after spending the past week thinking long and hard about his future, she felt she would do anything to fulfill her son's wishes. Indeed, in the hope that he would want to resume his studies after moving to Tokyo, she had already collected the materials for the equivalency exam. This made his proposal even more gratifying, and perhaps explained her clouded judgment.

Using the high-school equivalency exam as a pretext, Haruo played on his mother's love and demanded that his parents keep sending him money and stop interfering in his life. Mizue timidly suggested that he go to a cram school or take a correspondence course. Haruo curtly responded that it wasn't necessary. Bracing herself against his possible wrath, she asked whether he could really do it on his own. Before she could finish, he clicked his tongue, pointed at his laptop, and said, "This is all I need." He told her, with the vivid image of a crested ibis blazing in his mind, that he had already started studying online.

Although Haruo had absolutely no intention of studying for the exam, he was clearly interested in learning. He also harbored the vague feeling that as he poured his energies into the crested ibises he might free himself from his obsession with Sakura Motoki. And it was true, partially. As his search results for "Toya" led to Toya in Nagara-machi, Chosei County, Chiba Prefecture, and then to Togane City, as he discovered the background about Mei Mei, he felt consumed no longer solely by Sakura but by an impatient sense of duty. It burned within him even as he was talking with his mother. If he wanted to forget about Sakura, he would need to let that sense of duty guide him.

Did his mother know anything about their ancestors, he asked.

"Well, let's see... not really. You know what happened to your grandpa, and... I never asked your grandma anything more about it."

"Better not to know," he muttered, smiling insolently. When she asked why he wanted to know, he kept smiling and said nothing.

Suspicions roused, Mizue reverted to an obsequious expression and, in a faltering tone, tried to speak her mind. "Haru-chan, I think it's going to be hard for you here on your own. What if I came to see you every week? I'm worried it'll be tough for you to study and take care of yourself at the same time…"

At this, Haruo kicked over the trash can and threw a box of tissues at her. He couldn't stand the way she kept repeating things she had already said. Fearing he would kick her next, she retreated to the far wall and curled up like a pill bug. This made him even angrier.

"I'll kill you!" he screamed. He stopped spewing abuse at her when she promised to increase his monthly allowance and to stop meddling with his life. He got his allowance raised from 120,000 yen per month to 150,000. He had asked for 200,000, but his mother put her hands together, pleading for his forgiveness, because that amount was simply impossible. As a substitute, she suggested sending him money for his study materials and his clothing for each season as a separate payment. Haruo grudgingly accepted this offer.

Mizue picked up the objects thrown on the floor, then put the food she had brought into the refrigerator. She pulled three 10,000-yen bills out of her purse and placed them on the table. She went to the door and slipped into her shoes. Haruo, who had turned his attention back to his laptop as soon as their negotiations ended, couldn't be bothered to look away from the screen.

"Well then, I'm going."

He didn't reply. He didn't look up.

Mizue turned the door handle, but paused. She recalled how, a short while earlier, he had complained that if he actually liked himself, he wouldn't be living like this. She thought she would try to curry his favor one last time. "Haru-chan," she began, "if the money's not enough, let me know, OK? I'll do whatever I can. I'll try to make more money. Just be patient for the time being."

She looked quietly at his profile, waited five seconds for a response, which was not forthcoming, then left. As she went down the stairs, she thought she would go to the shrine to pray to Tenjin, the patron deity of learning.

●

Breed them, free them, or kill them. These were the three solutions that Haruo's brand of logic had led him to.

This was how he understood the situation:

The crested ibises are the sacrificial figures in "a script written by human beings." Further, there's no question that that scenario is part of the management of the state itself. Even as they speak of

"preservation" and "conservation," they have killed any number
of birds through human error.

Japan's breeding and conservation efforts had often
been criticized for their slow responses and flawed
methods. Their reputation was not good at all. Haruo
knew this much from his reading of the newspapers.

One article was especially thought-provoking. It
was a six-part weekly series published in the Mainichi
Interactive "Web Museum," beginning on March 23, 1997.
The author was Torao Honma, then-director of the Sado
Island Japanese Crested Ibis Conservation Center, and
it was a pessimistic account from beginning to end.
Honma doubted the effectiveness of the artificial breeding plan and considered the Environmental Agency's
various initiatives to capture all the wild birds a failure:

[…] The birds Yellow and Red died in June and July. Wounds
caused by being confined in narrow cages were infected with
staphylococcus. Two years later, in 1983, it was White. Her fallopian
tubes were blocked—something that rarely happens in the wild.
They discovered an egg lodged at the end of the fallopian tubes, but
only too late. She had been the most suitable mate for Green, and
the best female specimen, but they lost her because they allowed
her woefully inadequate exercise. The eggs that they were able to

salvage didn't hatch. Thanks to these multiple blunders, all they were left with were Green, Blue, whose right ankle joint had been injured before capture, and the aging Kin, who had long been in captivity. Three birds. The smallest number in history.

Nature or nurture? Public opinion seemed divided before the policy of capturing all the birds. In 1979, S. Dillon Ripley, then-president of the International Council for Bird Preservation, wrote to then-Prime Minister Masayoshi Ohira, asking him to capture all of the adult ibises and begin breeding them forthwith. The Environmental Agency could thus claim that the policy of total capture was supported by an international scientific consensus.

However, many feel that the breeding effort has only hastened the extinction of the crested ibis. After all, over the course of five years, four irreplaceable adult birds have died, one after another.

Chicks started being taken from their nests in 1967. The following year, a television-news helicopter startled a flock of twelve crested ibises, which unexpectedly abandoned their nests on Kurotakiyama and moved, en masse, one mountain over to Tachima. Near the coast, Tachima has a large population of kites and crows, which only accelerated the dying out of the ibises. In 1978, the government began collecting eggs, and in 1981 it began its effort to capture all the ibises in the wild. All of this just inflicted more suffering on the ibises, but to what end?

Haruo wrote in his diary:

Whether it's "nationality," "genetics," or "capture," whenever the government gets involved, it ends badly. Japan's governmental agencies have caused the ibises nothing but grief, and I feel that the harm done to the second-generation birds born in China—Yu Yu, Shin Shin, and Ai Ai—will be even worse. It will be no better than the days when they were hunted almost to extinction.

Being abandoned to the government's breeding and conservation efforts would only add insult to injury for the ibises. If it isn't handled well, they'll not only be spectacles stuck in cages, waiting to go extinct; they will also be used as experimental subjects for breeding and cloning techniques, and exploited to relieve the Japanese public's sense of guilt. That cursed name—*Nipponia nippon*—will drag the crested ibis to the bottom of a swamp.

In order truly to save the crested ibis in this country, the scientific name Nipponia nippon must be erased. The breeding and conservation effort, nothing more than a "script written by human beings," must be crushed. In particular, the Crested Ibis Preservation and Recovery Project must end. The ibises' only hope is to be freed from captivity, from exhibition, from experimentation, and rendered nameless.

Then what exactly should I do? Uncertain, Haruo lifted his hands from the keyboard. He had a faint idea of the answer, but for some reason he didn't want to pin it down just yet. His thoughts were in disarray; he felt uneasy. He couldn't find the words to express this emotion, so all that was left was to stop thinking altogether.

Haruo still wasn't aware that saving the ibises wasn't really his true motivation. Or perhaps he was dimly aware, but his conscience blocked him from acknowledging it. His feelings continued to be unsettled, and it would take a few more steps in his thinking before he arrived at a realization.

On January 26, 2001, Haruo woke up in the evening, as usual, went to the convenience store to pick up a bento, ate it, then went online. One of the sites that he usually checked, the Niigata Asahi.com Crested Ibis Diary, had been updated, so he caught up with the latest installments. One of the articles was about how Yu Yu and Mei Mei's feathers had started changing color because of breeding season. The end of the article explained that the ibises would not be on display from the first of February until the breeding season had ended during the summer.

He had not anticipated this.

In fact, the center had been closed to the public during the previous breeding season as well. Haruo had read about this earlier, but didn't know then as much as he knew now. He hadn't attached much importance to the fact, but jolted now by the revelation, he had to think quickly.

Haruo had never actually seen a crested ibis, and had not made any concrete plans to go to the Sado Island Japanese Crested Ibis Conservation Center. He just had the vague idea that he eventually would. He researched the birds at Sado, saw their miserable living conditions, felt anxious for their future, and wrote in his diary about finding some way to "save" them. But most of this was idle speculation; contrary to what he wrote in his diary, much of his thinking was completely detached from reality. Although he made his plans with great earnestness, once he went offline and turned off his laptop, his sense of the problem grew hazy. His passion never completely cooled, but the urgency faded when his overactive imagination was not fed.

If his sense of destiny had weakened, he might have been content to save the crested ibis and destroy "the script written by human beings" in the virtual realm of the cybersphere. That seemed likely, given who he was, but he didn't go there. He was thirsty for a real sense of accomplishment, and wouldn't allow himself any ersatz satisfaction. Although his goal was unclear, duty haunted him even when he was offline. His subconscious waited quietly for the moment when his will stepped out of the realm of the imagination into the real.

February 1. That meant that he would have to go to Sado Island within the next five days, or he wouldn't be able to the see the crested ibises for another six months. He was stung by the fierce immediacy. The problem was he hadn't worked out the details. He was filled with anxiety, feeling that if he didn't come up with a solution, his life would be rendered meaningless. He felt nauseated at the thought of spending the next six months fuming in this small apartment after having missed his chance. He thought his rekindled interest in the crested ibis had broken him out of his impasse, but in fact nothing had really changed, and perhaps wouldn't for the rest of his life.

Why had he spent the last three months and ten days researching the ibises with such tireless zeal? Would he abandon his mission in life now that he had found it? No! He resolved to figure out a solution as soon as possible.

He gave himself a five-day deadline, which galvanized his thinking and gave him a renewed sense of purpose.

"Why am I doing this?" he had asked himself with self-pity. He mulled this question over and over.

Something about his reasoning had been twisted. Finally he realized the root cause of his inexpressible disquiet: it was the idea that he was doing this all for the crested ibises. All this had started because he wanted to know the purpose of his own life, but at some point his interest shifted—to the ibises! He had lost sight of his original motivation.

He wrote:

I'm not such a good person, and I don't have it in me to dedicate myself to anything other than myself. Like the crested ibises, I'm trapped in a cage, and if I stay cooped up like this, my life will steadily lose all meaning and all worth.

All those little shits back home ran me out of town with the expectation that I would never amount to anything. No doubt about it. They want to pretend that I never lived in that town, that I never did what I did. They want to erase my existence and every memory of me.

They look down on me with contempt. They mistakenly think that if they could drive me away and leave me on my own, I would turn into a weakling and a coward. Well, they're idiots. I have always been a serious person. I get things done. Sakura's parents didn't understand that about me. In this day and age, it's easy to think you can rely on the police to keep you safe. They don't know what I'm capable of. Are they aware of how many times I've broken in to their house? They're complacent to the point of brainlessness. I can do anything I set my mind to. You think you can protect your precious daughter so easily? Fucking idiots!

But whatever. I don't care about Sakura anymore. I don't want to fall into the same trap again. I'll stop obsessing over her. It'll be hard to forget her, and the truth is my feelings haven't changed. But I need to put a lid on them. And now I can, because I've come to realize something: I have an important mission. This time, I have to see my goal clearly and make it happen. That's obvious to me now.

The only thing that matters to me is destroying that "script made by human beings." Saving the ibises was just a pretext. That's the truth. I'm doing this for myself. But I had to find myself alone first. My destiny left me in solitude.

Quitting school, being kicked out of the house, being locked up in this cramped shithole of an apartment—all of this was necessary for me to destroy the script. All of this was predetermined, meant to direct me to my life's purpose. From the beginning, it was my destiny.

It's not for the ibises. They are like my alter ego, but they've also triggered a major upheaval in my life. Of course I don't look down on the ibises. They're grand and noble creatures. I'm not like those government officials or scientists. What I mean to say is that only through my hands will the ibises have their revenge on this nation. With my help, they will dash the hopes of this country called Japan.

The sublime and endangered crested ibis is powerless, deprived even of the ability to escape or resist, turned into something like a puppet. It needs my help desperately. For my part, I have to use their plight to do the extraordinary, so that the world can't erase my existence. This is how fate has bound me to the ibises. In exchange for helping them get their revenge, the ibises will change my life, they will give my life meaning. This is how it has to be.

I'll make everyone in this country regret tossing me aside.

So Haruo admitted it: his desire for revenge, not the ibises' plight, was his driving force. His resentment at being kept from Sakura was now directed at the world, and took the form of wanting to destroy "the script made by human beings." His rage was indiscriminate. The hatred coursing through his body was propulsive.

It was this line of thinking that brought him to his three options: breed them, free them, or kill them. Any of these would delegitimize the state. Any one of them would empty out the cages in the Sado Island Crested Ibis Conservation Center, destroy the human script, and drive Japanese society to despair. The proponents of natural breeding might even shout for joy. His mind went in circles, tossing around these egomaniacal ideas as they occurred to him.

The first idea he had was to free them: releasing Yu Yu, Shin Shin, and Ai Ai—who had never once flown free—out of their cages. This solution was beautiful, benevolent, and extremely simple. At the same time, its impact on society would be profound.

Next, he considered breeding them: removing the ibises from Sado and caring for them himself. He knew this was mad, but the thought of living together with the ibises revived for him a long-abandoned image of utopia. It was precisely because it would be so difficult that realizing that dream would bring him great happiness.

Finally, Haruo thought of killing them. That would be the most effective way of destroying the human script, and the most practical. If they disappeared from the conservation center, the state would go on looking for them as long as they were alive. And Haruo knew well that if they were captured, they would go right back to the way they were before. If he wanted to cover all his bases, he had no choice but to kill them. He also assumed that the ibises would rather die with dignity than live in eternal imprisonment.

Each of these options had its merits. Each appealed to him.

Haruo harbored three illusions. One of them had been dashed early on, but the remaining two grew more detailed, concrete, and vivid with each passing day. He created a .txt file entitled "The Plan" based on those illusions. The first line of the file read: "The final solution to the *Nipponia nippon* problem."

●

Haruo shelved his plans to leave for Sado before February 1. It would be impossible to complete his preparations within five days, and he was no longer in any rush. His mission was clear to him now, and it was always a pleasure to ponder it. Writing "the final solution to the Nipponia nippon problem" filled him with the highest sense of purpose. The choice between releasing and killing the birds continued to vex him, but he even enjoyed pondering that dilemma as the days went by.

He decided to carry out the "final solution" after the center had reopened to the public in the summer; for the time being, he would let his ideas simmer and prepare for the voyage to Sado. He had a lot of time, so he methodically listed every detail he could think of and addressed them one by one.

It was during this process that he decided to arm himself.

He needed to find out what the punishment for his crime might be. He had no intention of being caught, but that was important knowledge to have in the worst-case scenario.

Was it even against the law to release or kill the crested ibises? If so, which laws were being broken? Haruo went online to find out.

According to the Red List of Threatened Species published by the Environmental Agency on June 12, 1998, the Japanese crested ibis falls into the "EW" (extinct in the wild) category. This is applied to species that "have been confirmed to have lived in Japan in the past and that survive because of breeding and cultivation, but are thought to be extinct in the wild."

Among flora and fauna whose habitat is Japan, the Japanese crested ibis has been certified as "extinct in the wild." It is protected by the Law for the Conservation of Endangered Species of Wild Fauna and Flora, which came into effect on April 1, 1993.

CHAPTER I: GENERAL PROVISIONS
ARTICLE 1 (PURPOSE)

In view of the fact that wild fauna and flora are not only important components of ecosystems but also serve an essential role in enriching the lives of human beings by forming an important part of the natural environment, the purpose of this Act is to secure biological diversity and conserve a healthy natural environment by ensuring the conservation of endangered species of wild fauna and flora, thereby contributing to securing wholesome and cultured lives for present and future generations of citizens.

In other words, this was the text of "the script made by human beings." "[E]ssential [...] in enriching the lives of human beings." "[S]ecuring wholesome and cultured lives for present and future generations of citizens." Haruo thought that these absolutely anthropocentric perspectives fit perfectly with the human script.

He read Article 9, "Prohibition of Capture," in Section 2, "Prohibition of Capturing Individuals and Transferring Individuals," which was in Chapter II, "Regulations on the Handling of Individuals." He also read Chapter IV, "Protection and Reproduction Programs," and Chapter VII, "Penal Provisions," in their entirety. These confirmed that he would indeed be punished for releasing or killing the ibises. The "script made by human beings" stipulated the following:

ARTICLE 9 (PROHIBITION OF CAPTURE)

A person must not catch, collect, kill, or damage (hereinafter collectively referred to as "capture") any live individual of a nationally rare species of wild fauna/flora or temporarily designated species (hereinafter collectively referred to as a "nationally rare species of wild fauna/flora, etc." in this Section and Article 54, paragraph (2)); provided, however, that this does not apply in the cases set forth below:

(i)   in case of capture with permission and as permitted under paragraph (1) of the following Article;

(ii) in case of capture of a live individual of a specified class II nationally rare species of wild fauna/flora for any purpose other than for the purpose of selling or distributing the individual;

(iii) in the cases specified by Ministry of the Environment Order as those where it is particularly necessary for the person to engage in the capture in order to earn a living and where the capture does not potentially affect the conservation of the species; or

(iv) if the capture is unavoidable for the protection of human life or body or for other unavoidable grounds specified by Ministry of the Environment Order.

CHAPTER VII: PENAL PROVISIONS
ARTICLE 58

A person who falls under any of the following items is punished by imprisonment for not more than one year or a fine of not more than one million yen:

(i) a person who has violated an order issued under the provisions of Article 11, paragraph (1) or (3), Article 14, paragraph (1) or (3), Article 16, paragraph (1) or (2), Article 18, Article 33-12, or Article 40, paragraph (2); or

(ii) a person who has violated the provisions of Article 9, Article 17, Article 20, paragraph (7), or Article 37, paragraph (4).

If Haruo carried out his plan, the penalty would be up to a year of imprisonment or up to a million-yen fine. He had no legal knowledge and couldn't tell if the punishment was heavy or light. But as far as he was concerned, less than a year of prison or a million yen didn't seem like such a big deal. He blithely assumed that he wouldn't even have to pay the fine. He had worried that, if caught, he might have to spend three or more years in prison, something he didn't think he'd be able to endure. So this new information emboldened him.

The next step in his planning was securing transportation on Sado Island.

He figured he'd need about two days there. He would spend the first night and the following day checking out the security and the surrounding area, then infiltrate the center on the second night.

Regardless of whether he was going to kill the ibises or release them, it had to be done at night. He wouldn't be able to take a bus at night, and he wanted to avoid any nosy taxi drivers who might report him to the police. There were no hotels or nightlife near the conservation center, so a high-school-aged tourist going there by himself at night would arouse suspicion.

In order for tourists to see the ibises, they first have to enter the museum at the Crested Ibis Forest Park in Niibo Village. The museum is next to the conservation center, and both buildings are surrounded by a forest. The museum is open from 8:30 a.m. to 5:00 p.m., but visitors must enter by 4:30 p.m. The museum is closed on Mondays (or on Tuesday if Monday is a holiday). It's also closed during the year-end holidays, from December 29 to January 3. The fee to enter, called an "Environmental Conservation Contribution," is 100 yen for elementary and middle-school students, and 200 yen for high-school students and older. This was all the information that Haruo could glean from the center's website.

Looking at the map, he could see that the center was in a remote part of Niibo Village, and there was nothing around it where he could kill time. According to the Niibo Village public homepage, you take the Niigata Kotsu Sado Bus (South Line) from Ryotsu Port to the nearest stop, which is at Gyoya. The ride takes about twenty minutes, and from there to the conservation center is a thirty-minute walk. It followed that, it would take a very long time to walk from the city center of Ryotsu, and that he would be exhausted on arrival. He didn't want to be seen walking there, and didn't think that he could walk that far.

He absolutely needed to preserve his strength until he entered the cage. He might need to do battle with the night guard or with security, and, once he got into the cage, it was unlikely that the birds would meekly allow themselves to be caught. If he tired himself out before the final stage of his plan, all of his efforts would be for nothing. Moreover, he still didn't have a firm grasp of the situation in Sado; he had to plan on the basis of hypotheticals. He also wanted to be able to move freely while inspecting the target area. The ideal was to be able to move around as inconspicuously and unhindered as possible. So the conclusion was that Haruo would have to drive himself. The problem was that he didn't have a driver's license. He would turn eighteen in a month, but he didn't want to have to go to driving school every day.

Another possibility was taking the last bus of the night to the Crested Ibis Forest Park, and hiding somewhere in the park until midnight.

He checked the Niigata Kotsu Sado Bus timetable online. The last bus left Ryotsu Port at 8:47 p.m., which meant that it should arrive at the Gyoya stop at 9:07. Assuming it took thirty minutes to walk to the Crested Ibis Forest Park from there, he would have to wait, hiding in the park for at least two hours until midnight.

That didn't seem too difficult, as long as he could find a suitable place to hide and had something to pass the time. There was no shortage of places to hide in a forest, and if he brought his laptop and mobile phone along, he could keep himself occupied. If their batteries held out, they could even help him finalize his planning.

Haruo considered this an expectedly good plan until a few days later, when he realized that he had overlooked some key points. The problem was that there was no way to escape. It would be dangerous staying in the park until dawn, and since he wasn't familiar with the terrain, his mobility would be limited. And if the police were called, he'd be arrested immediately.

It was back to the drawing board. After struggling with the problem for a time, he thought of bringing a folding bicycle to the island. This wasn't ideal, either: he wouldn't get far if police pursued him by car, and riding long distances would strain his stamina.

Desperation crept up on him as he rejected one idea after another. If he didn't stop thinking this way, his plan would never move forward. Settling for something less than perfect was the better part of wisdom, he thought. A bicycle had many advantages. If he started jogging every day, he could count on being in shape by the summer. So, for the time being, that was the plan.

●

Free them, or kill them? Nearly two months passed before he could decide.

A deep sympathy for the ibises made him want to set them free, while rationality demanded they be killed.

As long as this tension between sympathy and rationality persisted, he wouldn't be able to carry out his "final solution." This tension was Haruo's greatest fetter and his last safety valve.

The balance between sympathy and rationality that he had maintained over the last two months was not a product of the split personality that Haruo believed inhabited him. He was fueled by impatience and the sense of mission, and he wanted to avoid getting stuck in a dead end. At the same time, he was afraid of actually realizing his objective.

He often heard the voice of caution telling him not to do anything stupid, that he would not succeed. When he asked himself whether he could take the further step past the point of no return, he delayed answering.

"Further," because his banishment from his hometown had already made him an outcast, had shattered whatever plans he might have had for his life. This is not to say he had had any unusual dreams—all he knew were the conventions of society. His life plan amounted to going to a "first-rate" university, getting a job at a company listed in the First Section of the Tokyo Stock Exchange, and building a happy home with Sakura Motoki.

Although his exile was only a self-inflicted setback, he was bewildered by how far reality had deviated from his plans and expectations, and he resigned himself to the fact that after such chaos there would be no way to restore things to their original state. That's why he was serious about effecting a "major turnaround" in his life. He was sure that the opportunity to stage such a "major turnaround" would probably not come again. If he missed this chance, he would wind up a failure, in a place which he would never recover from. So he continued edging toward his target, the crested ibis, while maintaining that balance between sympathy and rationality.

Sooner or later, however, that balance would be tipped.

That happened on the morning of March 27, 2001, after he read the following article in the Society section of the *Yomiuri* online:

YU YU'S MATE MEI MEI LAYS EGG

On March 26, it was revealed that the female crested ibis Mei Mei has laid an egg at the Sado Crested Ibis Conservation center in Niibo Village in Niigata.

Center staff were able to see an egg in the nest via the CCTV monitor. Yu Yu and Mei Mei were taking turns sitting on the egg. If the egg is fertilized, it should hatch late next month.

Mei Mei was a gift from China, given in October of the previous year as a "bride" to Yu Yu, who was born in in Japan in 1999 as the first product of artificial breeding from ibises from China. The two have entered their first breeding season, and appeared to begin mating after the 20th of this month. (20:07, March 26)

Haruo's first reaction was rage.

He had already read an article on January 26 stating that the breeding season had begun, so none of this was exactly a surprise. But hearing that it had actually come to pass filled his mind with dark images that made his blood boil. It hadn't occurred to him before, but Yu Yu and Mei Mei seemed far too eager to perform as human beings wished. How could they be so unbothered, so unprincipled? For the first time, Haruo was angry at the ibises.

What he found especially shameful was that Yu Yu and Mei Mei continued to mate to their heart's content despite the precariousness of their situation. In fact, according to an article dated March 27 on the Niigata bureau homepage of the *Yomiuri Shinbun*, "the pair has been observed mating since the 20th, with daily intercourse confirmed since the 24th."

While he had been racking his brain, trying to find the right mode of transportation, Yu Yu and Mei Mei had been breeding. Even though it was breeding season, how could they be so shameless and insatiable? *And here I am*, he thought, *a virgin without a single sexual experience.* This was the wellspring of Haruo's rage.

Even though he constantly told himself that he was doing this out of self-interest and not out of an altruistic desire to save the birds, he kept expecting their gratitude. He wrote in his diary:

I felt pity for the ibises, and even felt that we were bound together by destiny. Yet as I spend months trying to figure out ways to set them free, Yu Yu and Mei Mei do nothing but have sex.

I feel betrayed. The fact is, I'm really disappointed. Yu Yu was only born two years ago; yet, without making the least effort, he has a mate in Mei Mei and can enjoy as much sex as he wants. Not only that, but he's free to flaunt his lewd behavior so that the human beings can "confirm" his "daily intercourse."

In short, the ibises have been completely domesticated. They really have. That much has been totally "confirmed." I didn't understand that until now. I felt a sense of brotherhood with the ibises. I still hoped that, even if they'd been turned into puppets, they still had some individuality, some rebellion within them. But they've become such degenerates that there's no hope of saving them. "Extinct in the wild," they said! The priceless crested ibis doesn't exist anywhere in the world now. It died out a long time ago. The ones living on Sado are nothing but worthless domestic fowl living carefree lives.

His criticism was wildly misdirected, but Haruo didn't have the intellectual tools to comprehend that. Indignation gushed forth as if from a burst dam, and this overwhelmed his reason. His preparations for Sado had forced him to make many sacrifices since the previous October; for the ibises now to be enjoying themselves was unacceptable. They had to be objects of pity, driven into terrible circumstances. The idea that these "priceless beings" should always seem weak and pitiful went from a preconception to a fixed idea in his mind, and he could not accept anything else. The more he identified with the ibises, the more narrow-minded and megalomaniacal he became.

Yu Yu's behavior particularly bruised his ego.

Since Yang Yang and Yo Yo were the parents of Yu Yu, Shin Shin, and Ai Ai, he could accept that they had had a lot of sex. But he had known of Yu Yu since Yu Yu was born; he still had an impression of his being practically a chick, and he was the one on whom he projected himself most readily. This made the contrast even more significant.

Haruo believed he himself had been as abstemious as he could over the past six months, but that wasn't the case at all. His main use for the internet, besides getting information about the ibises, was visiting porn sites. Masturbation was not only a daily habit, but the highlight of his day. Unfortunately for him, he didn't have a mating partner. He had to deal with his over-stretched libido alone.

How could Yu Yu, born so long after him, lose his virginity first? How did sexual opportunities come so easily to him, while for Haruo there wasn't a single one in sight? *Why are Yu Yu and Mei Mei getting it on so well, while Sakura Motoki and I were torn apart?*

Haruo envied Yu Yu. He knew their relationship was asymmetrical. The equation in which "poor Yu Yu" meant "poor me" now lay in ruins, and all that was left was "poor me."

Nothing could stop Haruo from resenting Yu Yu for that. This intense, childish jealousy filled Haruo with a raging sense of purpose. It didn't matter whether they were human beings or birds: when Haruo hated something, he wanted to kill it.

In that case, shall I kill them? I guess I'll kill them after all. Shall I stab Yu Yu again and again with the knife, dyeing his pure white plumage red with blood? Shall I just end it all, like that, with my own hands?

Just as he was pressing the return key on these words, his cell phone rang.

He picked the phone up and placed it against his ear. He heard the voice of Sakura Motoki.

This wasn't the first time; indeed, it happened often, so Haruo was not surprised. It wasn't her, it was some prick playing a prank on him. About half a month after he moved to Tokyo, the calls started coming once every two or three weeks. Recently they had increased to once a week.

Sakura's voice was probably a tape recording. She always said the same thing, so it had to be. "Please stop it already. Please stop doing this." He knew these words well, because she had said them to his face many times.

If it was only her voice saying those words, he could handle it, but the calls didn't end at that. The pleading was followed by stretches of silence, and, more recently, the caller then broke into a whole bunch of hateful bullshit. Haruo didn't know who the caller was; he wouldn't identify himself, and of course his face couldn't be seen. Haruo had a hunch he was Sakura's father, but the voice sounded more like his own father's.

The bullshit was always an update on Sakura, and it was malicious: Sakura had a new boyfriend, or she'd been raped, or she was sleeping around, or she liked this or that kind of sex play, or she looked pregnant, or she was still sleeping around after getting pregnant, or she was planning to get married to her high-school teacher, or she would keep sleeping around even after getting married. All fucking lies.

Haruo felt harassed, but he never refused to pick up the phone when it rang, and he never hung up on the caller. His parents and the prank caller were the only people who called him anyway. The lies upset him at first, but at some point he stopped caring. He even began to consider the calls his weekly entertainment. He had always been told he needed to work on his temper when he was younger; compared to then, he thought, he was a lot more patient now.

This prank call was no different from the others. The caller said that Sakura had been tormented over the past few days by a stalker. He added that she was sleeping around, as usual.

Even though he knew it was a lie, all lies, Haruo felt a twinge of anxiety when he heard that Sakura was being stalked. He had always worried that there was a risk of that happening. After making desperate pleas to Sakura's parents, he was forced into exile and he was no longer around to protect her. That was his only regret about moving to Tokyo. It was also the reason why his thoughts kept going around in circles.

He wondered whether he should go home and check on her.

On April 15, 2001, Haruo Toya turned eighteen. On this birthday, he made two important decisions.

First, he decided to get a driver's license. After going over his plan again, he couldn't banish his worries about the folding bicycle. There was no way it would suffice in a worst-case scenario. It would be dangerous to try to execute his plan while harboring such doubts, and he felt he needed the best plan possible in order to achieve his goal. He would need to wait until the next breeding season anyway. Getting a license was essential, so Haruo assigned himself the task.

The problem was commuting to the driving school; this could be solved by going to a driver training camp. That way he wouldn't get annoyed by the commute and wind up dropping out. The schedule was pre-configured, so there was no need to spend time making reservations. He could just focus on studying.

Choosing the school wasn't hard. He thought that the one in his hometown, rather than in Tokyo, would be best.

He entered the keywords "driver training institute," "camp," and "Yamagata" and the top hit was a website called Training Camp Reservation Center. Among the schools on the site, he chose the Murayama Driving School. It was near his old high school, and he knew the roads in the area like the back of his hand. It would be a lot less stressful to learn to drive there than in the city, and he'd be less likely to make mistakes. The shortest courses were fourteen days for automatic transmission, and sixteen days for manual. Adding the time spent taking the exam, he could get the license in twenty days, assuming he didn't fail the test.

Although it was a camp, there were single rooms so he would be able to live his usual lifestyle outside of classes. He thought it would be a good idea to devote the entire camp period to mission prep: driving school during the day, and physical training at night. As long as he didn't return to his parents' house, people wouldn't be able to hassle him; and if he disguised himself, he could probably walk around without being recognized. It wouldn't be that hard to catch a glimpse of Sakura from afar too. He might even be able to keep watch over her to his heart's content, like he did in the old days, when they were always together. He'd be killing two birds with one stone: learning how to drive, and making sure that Sakura was safe.

Haruo immediately contacted his parents and had his mother transfer the school fees. He applied to begin classes right after the holidays in May. At first, he wanted to start during the holidays, but he figured that the Motoki family might be away then, so he chose the later start date. Although he had sworn to forget all about Sakura, he was so happy to have the chance to protect her properly this time. He hoped that this would help calm his obsessive thoughts that kept going round and round.

Next, he set the date to carry out his mission. The "final solution to the Nipponia nippon problem" would take place on Sunday, October 14, 2001. In other words, he would fulfill his abiding wish half a year after his birthday.

He wasn't sure that he would be as motivated in six months as he was at this moment. He wanted to stay positive, but he also realized that his psychological volubility wasn't easy to predict or handle. Nonetheless, he vowed to forge ahead in the allotted time.

Even now, Haruo believed in only one thing: his destiny. He believed that as long as his intuitions about that destiny were true and not delusional, he would be going to Sado, no matter what happened.

On the morning of Saturday, October 13, he would leave his apartment and go to Sado Island, where he would sneak in to the ibises' enclosure the following night. On the day that Mei Mei was given as a gift to the Sado Crested Ibis Conservation Center by China, Haruo's destiny had been determined; he decided that, on the one-year anniversary of that event, he would kill Yu Yu.

The Joetsu Shinkansen Max Asahi 313 departed from Tokyo Station's platform 21 on schedule at 10:12 a.m.

Haruo sat in seat 29A, on the upper level of car number nine. The upper level was a Green Car, or first-class section, and seat 29A was a window seat at the rear end of the car. The three rows 27, 28, and 29 had only one seat on each of the left and right rows, so there was no chance that anybody would sit next to him. He was relieved that nobody besides the conductor would talk to him for the duration of the two-hour, five-minute ride to Niigata Station. He intended to sleep the whole way.

He hadn't slept at all the night before. This wasn't because of nerves or excitement; he had stayed awake deliberately to ensure that he wouldn't miss his train. He had worried that if he was awoken by some obtuse, overly friendly fellow passenger, he might snap and stab them with his knife. But that seemed pretty unlikely now.

His nocturnal lifestyle had remained unchanged, and he had continued doing research online. If anything had changed in the past six months, it was that he went out more and his body was a little more toned. He had been diligently working on his physical fitness to meet his goals. The day after he set the date to carry out his plan, he began walking and building up to a serious training regimen; since late August, he had been running almost every day. He would generally leave his room between 8 and 9 p.m., run through the deserted streets, and get back home at half past midnight. Even at night the intense summer heat lingered, but he wouldn't give up. He didn't run randomly around town, nor did he follow a fixed course. He often—though not always—carried his stun baton during these runs.

As his departure for Sado approached, Haruo had decided he needed to test the effectiveness of the stun baton. If he left it unused, there would be no way to know whether or not it was defective, and if it didn't work when he needed it, he would only make a fool of himself. Even though he knew it wasn't lethal, no way was he going to try it out on himself. And since he would need to react instantly when the time came, he needed practice handling it. He needed a test subject.

The first was a vagrant in an underpass. The next was a vagrant in the park. The third was a vagrant he encountered on the sidewalk. This was enough to confirm the baton's effectiveness, but Haruo wanted more. The more he used the stun baton, the more intense was the rush he got from attacking random unsuspecting people. He got hooked on the thrill, and he didn't want to stop. These were practice runs for the real battle to come, but they were also a stress release.

After the fourth test subject, he started targeting students and salarymen who'd drunk too much. He would ambush them at the train station, or find some stumbling fool in the entertainment district and follow him, then decide what to do next. If the voltage multiplication circuit burnt out, the stun baton would be useless, so he didn't use it every time; sometimes he just beat his victims. The baton can inflict a heavy blow, enough to break bones if done with full force. He began to like the sensation of beating people, the power in his hands.

He didn't confine his forays to his own neighborhood. He would get on the train and choose a neighborhood a few stops away. He would never go to the same neighborhood twice, and he let time pass between visits. Because he was so vigilant, the police never stopped and questioned him. However, this made it difficult to find a suitable target, and sometimes his targets would fight back. Nonetheless, all of this was useful experience and helped him to fine-tune his plans.

Things took a turn in mid-September. After he had whacked his eighth test subject, his activities made the news and were reported on television. Haruo had to give up on finding a ninth.

According to one victim's testimony, the assailant was a male in his late teens or early twenties, of medium build. The reporter pointed out that the scenes of the crimes were spread out, which suggested that there was more than one perpetrator. A different news program charted the dates and times of the attacks; for some reason, there had been thirteen incidents, which Haruo found puzzling. A copycat? How could that be if this was first time the attacks were reported?

Fortunately, no witnesses came forward. Haruo was aware that the arrest rate for the police was declining every year, and with many unsolved cases they were short-handed. He thought little of the police and assumed he would never get caught. Yet, at the same time, he could not rest easy: his stun baton, if somehow retrieved, could be traced back to the seller, and although he had the cover of darkness, a few of his victims got a good look at his face. Plus, thanks to the copycat attacks, the police were now more on the alert.

If he got arrested now, he would of course not be able to go to Sado, and everything would have been for naught. Haruo brooded over this, regretting how stupid he had been. He also wondered whether he, in his heart of hearts, actually wanted the mission to fail. He hated having to acknowledge such weakness, so he tried to overcome these troubling thoughts and quickly returned to daydreaming. He was upset for two or three days, and even stopped his nightly runs.

Then he got lucky. Five days after the first news reports, the copycat was arrested. He was a nineteen-year-old who had failed his university entrance exams and was living alone in an apartment in Tokyo. He hadn't seen Haruo committing his crimes; he was just unlucky enough to have embarked on a similar spree at the same time. Conveniently for Haruo, the police and media seemed to think he was responsible for all thirteen incidents.

Most students who fail the exams go to cram school to prepare to take them again the following year, but that wasn't the case with this young loser. His landlord told the TV news that he never went out during the day, seemed to be a *hikikomori* shut-in, and would occasionally start screaming. His mother lived one neighborhood over and came to look after him daily. On the rare occasions when the landlord encountered him, the boy wouldn't say a word. No friends came to visit, and his room was like a pigsty and stank. The landlord's face was pixelated, to disguise his identity, and he sometimes lowered his voice, but his implication was clear: it was only a matter of time before the young man did such a thing.

Although Haruo could see the similarities between them, he felt no sympathy for him. He dismissed him as the dregs of humanity, while his own self-confidence bubbled over. Even though their situations might have been similar, he felt there was evidence that his destiny would prove them as different as night and day. For Haruo, this outcome only confirmed for him his mission and that destiny was on his side.

Now that a perpetrator had been caught and the attacks had ceased, talk of the crimes would die down and the media would soon stop reporting on them. Even so, the police investigation might still be ongoing. To be safe, Haruo decided to do his running in the morning instead of at night.

He also took this as an opportunity to change his appearance. He shaved his head and trimmed his eyebrows. He went to Harajuku, fashion magazine in hand, and bought an outfit in the latest style. He had no interest in pop culture; it was a disguise to throw off the investigation, as well as a rite of passage toward the execution of his mission. He greeted October 13 with the palpable sense that he had become a different person. His confidence in himself—and his overconfidence—were back.

It was Haruo's first time taking the Joetsu Shinkansen, riding a double-decker car, and sitting in a Green Car seat. None of this stirred any strong feelings in him. He had paid 27,520 yen for a round-trip ticket. He had no idea whether that was expensive or cheap; it was his parents' money. He chose the bullet train because it was faster and less tiring than taking a bus or renting a car. On the way back from Sado, he was supposed to board the Asahi 310, which departed from Niigata Station at 10:10 a.m. on October 15 and arrived at Tokyo Station at 12:20 p.m.

He reclined his seat and stared out the window for a while. He drank orange juice. He closed the curtain, pulled the brim of his pork-pie hat down to block out the light, and closed his eyes.

His backpack was at his feet, a precaution against theft while he dozed. It didn't contain travel necessities. It was packed with a jumble of weapons and high-tech gear and had to be handled with care. It contained only items essential for his mission: a laptop, a cell phone, the stun baton, pepper spray, two sets of handcuffs, the survival knife, two sets of ultra-thin rubber gloves, a sports towel, a pipe wrench and screwdriver, a flash-light, a set of lock picks, a notepad, a ballpoint pen, worn-out sneakers, a balaclava, and overalls. Whatever else he needed he would procure locally.

The lock picks were essential for opening the cage. Haruo had purchased the set two years earlier, along with an instruction manual, and had experience using it. As long as you didn't rush, it was possible to pick within ten minutes the most common types of pin-tumbler and disc-tumbler cylinder locks used in Japan. He had spent the days before his departure practicing on his apartment door. If the locks weren't the cylinder type, or for some reason he couldn't unlock them, he could use the pipe wrench and screwdriver to pry the cage open.

The rubber gloves were so he wouldn't leave any fingerprints, but since he would be leaving footprints however lightly he stepped, he bought some used sneakers. He bought the balaclava and overalls at the same used-clothing shop. He chose dark blue for both, thinking it would blend into the darkness. If he got splattered with blood, he would go to the harbor before dawn and throw the clothes into the water.

He had set aside 150,000 yen for expenses. He had to pay for the round-trip Shinkansen ticket, a round-trip ticket from Niigata Harbor to Ryotsu Harbor, one night in a hotel, two days of car rental. That came to a total of 65,000 to 67,000 yen. After subtracting the cost of meals and anything else he bought there, he would still have around 60,000 yen left.

Haruo thought that if he accomplished his mission and made it back to Tokyo safely, he would celebrate, but he couldn't think how exactly. Fine dining, sightseeing, shopping—he felt little desire for such things.

He had been so focused for the past six months on finding a "final solution to the Nipponia nippon problem" that he wondered if he had turned into a bore. But he knew he hadn't completely dried up inside. His sexual desire, for example, was what one would expect of a someone in his late teens. But Haruo, who was still a virgin and had never set foot in a brothel, couldn't imagine, except in the most abstract terms, what 60,000 yen could buy him in the way of sex. Adult videos and outright pornography—he consumed these things, but they had no anchor in his reality. He was also reluctant to pay to have sex with a stranger. Haruo was naïve in that sense, and very simple in his desires.

If he could do anything with that 60,000 yen, it would be to see Sakura again. But that was something that money couldn't buy. No matter how hard he worked, or how many good deeds he did, even if he grew into a person trusted by all around him, he would never be able to see Sakura Motoki again. No matter how hard you try, you cannot resurrect the dead, or exchange with them even the most trivial of pleasantries.

●

He usually went to bed in his apartment at around this time, so he thought he would be able to fall asleep easily, but when he closed his eyes, he didn't feel sleepy at all. Although he generally didn't fall asleep in the sitting position, he grew increasingly irritated at how worthless the Green Car seat had proven to be. This made it even harder to fall asleep.

Realizing that the conductor hadn't checked his ticket yet, he decided to give up on sleep and took off his hat. Turning his head, he noticed a petite girl in her early teens sitting in seat 29D, which had been empty when the train pulled out of Ueno Station. She was quietly staring out at the passing scenery. Taking her cue, he opened his curtain and looked outside his window. He figured he would while away the time that way, waiting for sleep to come.

The conductor announced himself in the Green Car as the train left Omiya Station. Haruo was getting his tickets out of his wallet when the conductor began remonstrating with the girl about something. Apparently she didn't know that the upper level was for Green Car ticket-holders only. If the girl wanted to stay where she was seated, she'd need to pay the Green Car fare. The girl looked at the conductor blankly, protesting that she'd already bought a ticket before eventually realizing her error. Blushing, she rose to move to the unreserved car. Her right hand was pressed to the back of her bowed head in embarrassment. She was traveling only with an orange sling bag.

Haruo couldn't sleep the entire journey to Niigata. He was too tense about his impending mission, too agitated by travel.

He emerged from the station around 12:20 p.m. Not only had he not slept, he hadn't had a decent meal since the night before. But he was booked for a jetfoil leaving at 1:00 p.m., so he didn't have time to spare. He took a taxi to the Sado Kisen Terminal. It took about seven minutes and the fare was 1,090 yen.

The jetfoil, called the *Mikado*, was scheduled to arrive at Ryotsu Port at 2:00 p.m. Thinking that he could have a meal as soon as he arrived on Sado, he bought a half-liter bottle of a sports drink. He'd been terribly thirsty on the Shinkansen, but taking fluid now on an empty stomach seemed to sate his appetite.

He completed the boarding procedures by filling out the passenger registry with a false name, age, and address, then proceeded to the waiting room. Fewer than half the seats were occupied, and most of the people there seemed to be locals. Haruo went to the back of the waiting room and put his bag down in a seat next to him. A television was showing the NHK channel. The electronic departure board indicated seats were still available for the *Mikado*. It seemed that at this time of year not many tourists were going to Sado, even on weekends.

On a large sculpted pillar, painted red and black, to the right of television, a placard read, "Kwakiutl Indian Totem Pole. Commemorating the Completion of the Bandaijima Ferry Terminal, July 1981. Donated by Boeing Marine Systems, made by Tony Hunt." In smaller type was an explanation of the meaning of the totem pole: the killer whale represented "great power and good fortune," while the sea eagle represented "strength and friendship." Haruo was perplexed that a totem pole should be in an embarkation waiting room.

Behind him there was a poster of two crested ibises. The wording, in red, at the top read "Sado: The Island of Crested Ibises." Haruo's heart began to race when he realized that in a little more than an hour he would arrive at his long-desired destination and meet the ibises face to face. All of the scenes he had seared into his imagination over the past months would become reality. Haruo looked at the totem pole again, and thought, *"Great power and good fortune," and "Strength and friendship." Maybe these should be my mottoes.*

A few minutes before 1:00 p.m., passengers for the *Mikado* began to line up at the gate. Haruo was getting in the back of the line when somebody stumbled and bumped into him. Reflexively, he turned around, and was surprised to see that it was the petite teenage girl from the Shinkansen. "I'm very sorry," she said softly, placing the palms of her hands together. "Please excuse me." Haruo acknowledged her apology with a silent nod.

The jetfoil had 260 passenger seats, split between two levels. Haruo's reserved seat was 13A, to the left and rear of the lower deck. It was a window seat, so he could have enjoyed a view of the sea during the trip, but he wanted to sleep instead. A plump older woman sat down in the seat one over and smiled at him in greeting, but he ignored her and closed his eyes.

Before his preoccupation with securing transport on Sado, Haruo's biggest worry had been deciding how to get there from the main island of Honshu. Traveling long distances by air or sea, with his life in others' hands, made Haruo anxious. The worst-case scenario filled him with overwhelming fear. When the nuclear U.S. Navy submarine USS *Greenville* collided with the *Ehime* Maru, a training fishery ship from Ehime Prefecture, off the coast of Hawaii on February 9 of that year, he was shaken to his core. He also recalled that Sakura Motoki was born on September 1, 1983, the day when the Korean Air jet was shot down by a Soviet interceptor plane.

Although he dreaded boats and planes equally, he had decided to go by sea. Boats seemed less dangerous in general, but he was also persuaded by an article about jetfoils on the Sado Kisen website. The jetfoil, it said, was of a fully submersible hydrofoil design and was "the ultimate high-speed boat, using the latest in aerospace technology." "It can rise 3.5 meters above rough seas and travel at 80 kilometers per hour." "The computerized control system, similar to those used in aircraft, allows it to travel at 80 km/h over rough seas without pitching or rolling," and "with an emergency stopping distance of 180 meters, it's safer than conventional vessels." It even had "shock absorbers that keep passengers from being jolted if the boat strikes a floating object." Haruo was reassured, and marveled at what a wonderful vessel it must be. He even began looking forward to the journey.

It was true: the ship didn't rock or sway, and it slid over the surface of the water. If he felt bored but couldn't sleep, he could watch one of the televisions installed throughout. Or he could pass the time by comparing the speed of the boat, which was periodically displayed on the screens, with the view passing by outside. Passengers were required to wear seat belts while the boat was in motion, so he couldn't get up and walk around except to go to the toilet; but he couldn't complain since the trip only lasted an hour.

Despite that, it was difficult for Haruo to calm down. The ship didn't sway, but Haruo couldn't see land, which left him quite anxious. Being stuck in his seat was especially hard on his nerves, and whatever drowsiness he might have felt disappeared.

There'd be no end to it if he started listing all the unpleasant feelings swirling within him. He needed to distract himself. It wasn't easy for him, though, to shift gears like that and stop imagining the worst. He started to worry whether he had forgotten something, so he opened his backpack, which was in the seat next to him, and was relieved to see everything there. It was packed with weapons, but since there was no baggage inspection, he had been able to carry it aboard without trouble. It occurred to him that, if he wanted, he could even seajack the jetfoil. His mood darkened. He was suddenly filled with hatred for the world, with heinous fantasies. *Well then, what should I do?*

He wanted to free himself from the uncomfortable seat and return to land so strongly that he felt the urge to bolt. But he did his best to repress the urge and simply allowed his intense emotions to fester. He had come this far; he wasn't going to screw it up now. His destiny and desires would not allow him to stop just short of his target, to end his voyage without even getting a glimpse of his goal. Discomfort and the impulse to do something reckless swelled within him, but he was able to get himself under control by telling himself that this was the great mission of his life.

All he had to do was wait another day, and by tomorrow night he would make all the smug assholes—not just here, but throughout Japan—suffer. The people around him could never guess that a kid like him was thinking such bold and daring thoughts. How terrible, they would lament, that we didn't stop him before he killed Yu Yu! *Especially that old lady sleeping over there: if word spread that I was the one who killed Yu Yu, she'd blubber about how powerless and terrible she felt.*

He looked stonily into the faces of all of the other passengers around him. He kept staring at them, whether they looked back or not, no matter who they were. It was an escape from his discomfort, but it was also more preparation for his mission, a way to fortify his sense of self.

Among the enemies who surrounded him, only one had a familiar face.

He was flustered by her and looked away; when he looked again three seconds later, she was in profile. The petite girl from the train was sitting in seat 15D, to the far-left side of a row at the back of the center section. She was drowsily watching one of the televisions.

They made eye contact for an instant; Haruo blinked and looked down, then looked at her again. She did the same, as if she were his mirror image, then observed his expression through upturned eyes. She seemed to think he was staring at her because he was angry she bumped into him earlier. This made her uncomfortable. Haruo faintly realized that it wouldn't be good if he seemed too interested in her, so he pretended to look up at the ceiling.

Ten minutes later, when he looked over at seat 15D, she was sound asleep.

As he stared at her sleeping face, he realized that they had been together since morning. What were the odds that they'd be going to same place, and taking the same train and boat? His thoughts soon took their usual, delusional turn.

They had crossed paths too many times over the past three hours for it to be mere coincidence. She had spoken to him, if only to apologize. They had to have some kind of connection. That was his interpretation, at least. He didn't know, though, what kind of a connection it was, or where it would lead them. In any case, some kind of destiny was at work: they had taken the same train, the same boat, and they were going to the same Sado Island.

Perhaps because this kind of fantasy was a part of his daily life, it had a moderately relaxing effect and calmed him down. As with the crested ibises, his feelings were sincere, but he also didn't completely believe in it. He *did* believe in destiny—that much was consistent. But he was also able to analyze the situation dispassionately. It was like a subtle shift in disposition.

Yet there was always the possibility of short circuits and confusion. She gradually became the object of desires he had cultivated over many years. Or perhaps she already had become so on the Shinkansen. She somehow resembled—no, she was the spitting image of—Sakura Motoki. They were twins!

Except that she didn't wear glasses, she didn't braid her hair, her complexion wasn't as light, and she didn't have drooping eyes. Their only shared traits were their short height and round faces, but that was enough for Haruo. They were similar enough to give this girl an aura of danger, to drive him mad, and to arouse his protective instincts. For all he knew, she was Sakura's ghost in a slightly altered body. Perhaps Sakura's ghost, in this physical embodiment, had come to accompany him on his mission.

Sakura was self-effacing like that. She was such a good girl...

●

Haruo and Sakura first spoke to one another in April 1997. It was the first day of eighth grade, in homeroom seven. The year before, they had been in homerooms on either side of their middle school. In elementary school, they had been in different school districts. A reshuffle put them in the same homeroom, and a lottery seated them next to one another. The physical distance that had separated them for years was gone in a day.

Their first conversation was about his last name.

"T-O-Y-A?"

"Yes. T-O-Y-A."

"Toya? Toya. That's an unusual last name. Do people ever tell you that?"

"Well... actually, no."

"Really? I've never heard that name before. I think it's unusual. I don't know, maybe I'm just ignorant. I've never even seen that character before," she said, pointing at the kanji for "crested ibis" on his name tag.

Haruo felt flustered, but, being careful not to stutter, he explained to her what the character meant. That is, he shared with her something which he was proud about, and which nobody else had appreciated.

It was obvious to anyone watching how excited he was at that moment. He could barely contain his joy. He was elated that she said his name was "unusual." She even smiled as he told her his long-winded story; this was a first for Haruo.

The chitchat about his name continued for a while.

"What month were you born?" he asked.

"Huh? Why?"

"I was born in April."

"Uh…"

"Weren't you also born in April or May?"

"No," she replied. "I was born in September. Why?"

"I mean, your name… 'cherry blossom.'"

"Oh, right. Yeah, I see…"

"I was born in the spring, so my parents named me Haruo, with the kanji for 'spring' and 'born.' Parents are so simpleminded! They don't have any original thoughts. Naming me Haruo because I was born in spring. I mean, come on! Making fun of a newborn baby! Their firstborn son too. I thought you had to be the same… named Sakura because you were born in spring. It has a lot of nice associations, Sakura-chan. But September? Which day in September? What day of the month were you born?"

This was the longest, and most pleasant, conversation they ever had. They never had an opportunity to talk after that. It was the first and last time that Sakura spoke to him with friendliness and warmth. And it was the first time he'd been able to talk with a girl he had a crush on, the first time to have a girl appreciate what a rare name he had. This made him so giddy that he wound up talking too much. He wanted so badly to have her like him that he started talking about things she hadn't even asked about. As his torrent of words poured out, he lost any ability to notice that she clearly had become uncomfortable.

Ever since the seventh grade, Haruo had felt the stirrings of first love every time he passed the pale, bespectacled, petite girl with braids from homeroom eight, whether in the hallway, the gym, or on the grounds of the school. After he found out that her name was Sakura, he wrote "Sakura-chan" in his diary day after day. He only called her that in his diary and in his heart; when he passed her at school, all he could do was stare at her. So, when they moved up to the eighth grade and found themselves in the same homeroom and seated next to each other, and when the first thing she did was to ask about his name, and when he was actually able to call her "Sakura-chan," it was a completely unanticipated moment of joy.

He wrote in his diary, in red ink, that the first day of eighth grade was the happiest day in his life, one that he would never forget. He also believed that this happiness would not only continue for the rest of his life, but that it would deepen with each passing day. In Haruo's mind, as long as they were seated together, they would only grow closer. Except that the homeroom teacher never promised that the seating arrangement would stay fixed through the year, and indeed, during seventh grade, seating was changed every two months. Haruo's optimism—or rather, his fantasy—led only to disappointment.

On the first Monday in June, the seats in eighth grade, homeroom seven, were rearranged. Haruo didn't sit next to Sakura after that.

As they entered the second term, troubles arose in quick succession. Other students began to bully him. Three boys that he'd never gotten along with conspired to knock him around almost every day, in ways large and small. After the school's culture festival in late October, their nastiness grew vile. Between classes they stole his notebook, a notebook that he had filled with his reveries about "Sakura-chan." After school that day, before chorus rehearsal, when Haruo had gone to the staff room to print out some music, the bullies stood up and read out loud to everyone the contents of Haruo's notebook—in particular, his sexual fantasies about "Sakura-chan," including watching her urinate and shaving her pubic hair. Then they tore the notebook to scraps, scattering the pieces around the classroom. When Haruo came back and discovered what they'd done, he went mad. He bit off the earlobe of one boy and pulled out tufts of his hair; the other two ran off, so Haruo threw their backpacks into the sewer. The bullying was transformed into a vendetta that lasted until winter break.

After a three-day suspension, Haruo returned to school. Although a few classmates had probably guessed Haruo's feelings for Sakura, everybody now knew exactly what they were, and the atmosphere in the classroom was never what it had been. Sakura acted like a bystander to all that had happened, as if she were not the "Sakura-chan" whose name had filled his notebook. Haruo thought that if he faltered now, he would be defeated; he had to take the battle to his enemies. But he was overwhelmed with heartache. He couldn't call out to Sakura and explain why he had written those words. For her part, "Sakura-chan" would not take a step closer than ten feet from him, and she made sure their eyes never met.

During lunch recess on the rooftop one day, he saw her crying and her friends consoling her. Apparently, some male students had made fun of her. Haruo immediately went into action and pushed one of the boys down a flight of stairs. When Sakura learned about this, she went up to Haruo, her eyes puffy with tears. "Please stop it!" she screamed, then stormed off. It seemed the closer Haruo tried to get to her, the farther away she ran from him.

They were in the same class, so it was impossible for her to avoid all contact. Haruo tried as often as he could to get closer than ten feet to talk to her, but to little avail. With the cooler weather in December, she might come around, he hoped. But even when snow was piling up, "Sakura-chan" would not let him near her. Girls at school called him "super-perverted," and one of Sakura's friends actually said to his face, "Drop dead, you heartless creep!" But Haruo turned a deaf ear to all that. He may or may not have been a pervert, but he was not heartless.

His final year of middle school was one bleak day after another. He and Sakura had been assigned to different homerooms, and there was no way to bridge the distance. Like the previous year, it was a long, barren period when all he could do was wait for the chance that their paths might cross. Haruo didn't give up hope, however, and believed that time would offer up a solution. He hoped that once they went to high school, with a different environment and student body, her attitude toward him would soften. In his usual one-sided fashion, he imagined that if she just put aside her own preconceptions and other people's opinions of him, if she just got to know him, she would see his good qualities and fall for him. But in order for that to happen, they needed to attend the same high school—and that simple detail proved to be Haruo's tragic stumbling block.

He didn't fail his high school entrance exam. He even got into the high school of his choice. The part that tripped him up was something more basic. Even if he studied as hard as students taking the university entrance exam, he'd never be admitted to an all-girls high school.

That was tough enough, but it wasn't the only snag in his plans. When he found out that she was going to an all-girls school, he could have chosen to attend a high school near hers. Instead, he chose to attend the school that best fit his academic ability, which meant getting on a train going in the opposite direction. The schools were so far apart that there were two cities between them. This triggered Haruo's downfall.

Before, all he had to do was go to school, and Sakura would be there. No matter that she avoided him and regarded him with contempt, at least he could see her face and hear her voice every day. But once he entered high school, it was as if Sakura had disappeared. The thought that this would continue, not for a day or two, but for weeks, months, years, drove Haruo to distraction. He couldn't sit still.

He lost himself in memories of their one conversation, reliving the moment over and over. What was important was having the right priorities. Being with Sakura was the aim of his life. As long as he aspired to that and that alone, as long as he thought seriously about how to achieve it, as long as he was single-minded and poured his heart and soul into it, then it was possible that one day they would walk together, hand in hand. Driven into a corner by crisis and yearning, Haruo allowed his delusions free rein.

This was how he began stalking Sakura Motoki.

●

Haruo did most of the things that society considers to be stalking. He started shadowing her during the summer break after his first year of high school; midway through the first term of his second year, he stopped going to his school altogether. He couldn't rest unless he knew everything about her, so he tried indiscriminately to find out everything he could. Every day spent in pursuit of "Sakura-chan" fulfilled him, and he told himself he was doing the right thing. But the pleasure was empty and soon ended. As time passed, his pursuit of her became increasingly painful.

He couldn't feel her essence if he only observed her in public. The true "Sakura-chan" would only come out when she was alone in her bedroom. Perhaps then, she might reveal her true feelings toward her eighth-grade classmate, Haruo Toya. Maybe she actually liked him, but was so embarrassed after the notebook incident that she kept her distance, and unfortunately she never had the chance to tell him so before they went to separate high schools.

He tried calling her on the telephone. But he never got through, despite the many times he tried. Her father would pick up the phone and hang up on him, repeatedly, until one day his calls suddenly stopped going through altogether. He had to think of some other way to reach her.

He got the lock-pick set in the mid-October of his first year of high school. That was his first time buying something online. The following month, he bought a listening device with a transmitter and a receiver from the same vendor. He bought it all with his monthly allowance, supplemented with the 1,000-yen bills he stole from the soba-shop cash register every day.

He carefully studied the lock-picking manual and practiced late into the night, every night, on some Miwa cylinder locks he had also acquired. He wasn't naturally dexterous, so he had to practice until his fingers literally bled, but by winter vacation his technique was almost perfect. The types of locks that could be picked were of course limited, but, as long as he could get through the Motoki family's front door, that was enough.

When he discovered that the Motoki family was leaving on a winter vacation, Haruo put his skills to the test. He picked the front door lock easily, then found his way to Sakura's bedroom, where he wanted to plant a bug. But entering her inner sanctum filled him with a nervousness and excitement that was overpowering, making it difficult to find a good spot to install the device. He finally calmed down and managed to set up the bug, then went to the laundry basket hoping to find a pair of Sakura's worn panties. It was impossible to tell which belonged to "Sakura-chan" and which to her mother. After settling on a likely candidate, he rushed home, not taking anything else. He was filled with contentment.

By the standards of common sense, Haruo had by this point already gone mad. But his true breaking point didn't come until some months after bugging Sakura's room. To be more precise, his mental state began to crumble after reading Sakura's diary. He learned that she was in love with her math teacher.

The listening device was not only not a great success: it led to disaster. Even though the snowfall had been less than in previous years, the time Haruo spent outdoors in the Yamagata night air was akin to self-mortification. After three consecutive days of it, he developed a high fever. Running a temperature of 102 that didn't subside by morning, he went to the doctor, who told him he had influenza. He was not to set foot out of the house for a week.

He gave up on the listening device. He couldn't make out what was being said anyway. Instead, he would sneak into "Sakura-chan's" room again. The opportunity didn't come easily. During spring break, he approached the house twice, but when he saw police on patrol, he thought it too dangerous to proceed. It was during the Golden Week holidays in early May, when most families go away for three or four days, that he achieved his goal. He broke in on May 3.

Even before he got in the front door, Haruo had a single target. A serious girl like "Sakura-chan" would certainly keep a diary. After all, even he wrote in his diary every day without fail, and he could just imagine what kind of delicate feelings, recorded in minute detail, would be found in hers.

He pulled off his shoes and bounded up the stairs. The diaries—there were four volumes of them—were so easy to find that he thought they must be a decoy. In the bottom drawer of her desk, there they were—bound volumes that covered the first term of seventh grade to the winter term of tenth grade. She must have taken the current volume for eleventh grade with her on vacation.

"Sakura-chan," he was gratified to see, was as precise as he had imagined. Haruo stayed in the Motoki house for the whole day, reading through every page of her diaries. This allowed him to survey the changes in her thoughts and feelings in the time since he had first met her. Getting to know her true nature gave him a sense of fulfillment, as if he was somehow enlarged by it. As he turned the pages, he murmured things to himself like, "I knew it," and "I always understood you," and "I always saw what was happening." Every word of her diaries seared itself into his memory, into his heart. He was excited, thrilled, but when he got to the last volume, his excitement turned to disgust.

He didn't find the words "Toya" or "Haruo" anywhere, but references to "him" and "the dung beetle" and "x" were followed by torrents of abuse. This didn't faze him, honestly. He was prepared for it, and confident that he could change her opinion of him. Even when he read that she had fallen in love with her teacher, he didn't lose hope. Such things were practically an epidemic among high-school girls. But it disgusted him, and as he stole out of the house, he resolved not to let her disease progress any further.

The math teacher in question was the quintessential middle-aged dullard with a wife and two children. Haruo found out where he lived and distributed a slanderous flyer in his neighborhood. It read: "Lewd Teacher Propositions Students." He made silent phone calls to the teacher's home in the middle of the night and repurposed his flyer as a "complaint" that he sent to Sakura's school. When this failed to produce results, he tried to appeal directly to Sakura's parents, who shunned any contact with him. All the while, he monitored the Motoki family's comings and goings and let himself into the house to continue reading Sakura's diary whenever he was sure they weren't home. Needless to say, he followed her whenever he could, and did what was necessary to keep suspicious or bothersome individuals away from her. At some point, he came to believe he was her bodyguard, like Kevin Costner in the film of that title. Her parents seemed uninterested in the fact that she was on the verge of being seduced by a married teacher, while the incompetent police seemed incapable of addressing a brewing scandal. Who but he could protect her from evil? "Sakura-chan" was like a graceful crane in a garbage dump, surrounded by roving bands of perverts and thugs here in the hinterlands, and Haruo was her guardian angel.

So, he continued diligently to "guard" her. But the closer he got to her, the further she pulled away from him, like a magnet repelled by another with the same polarity. It seemed this would never change. Things got worse instead of better, and he was getting fed up. He had done everything he could to keep her teacher away from her, and he had run interference for her when any boy showed interest. But her disgust for Haruo was reaching new heights, and the entries in her diary were getting harder and harder to stomach. He wanted to be done with the whole affair, but he couldn't control his impulses, and Sakura's refusal to pay him any attention frustrated him deeply and only made him want her more. Still, he at least could stop the breaking-and-entering foolishness, and so he stashed his lock pick set in the drop ceiling of his brother's room. When it got late at night, however, he couldn't keep himself from going out and prowling around the Motoki house. He was no longer acting of his own volition.

And then reality, as if in response to his own inner turmoil, put the brakes on. At the end of July, Haruo was placed in police custody because of his late-night prowling. His stalking had come to an end.

That was in fact the third time he had been taken into custody. The Motoki family had complained to the police, who in turn had contacted Haruo's family repeatedly about the matter. But his more serious offenses had not come to light and, perhaps because he was a minor, the police didn't take the situation very seriously. Haruo was sent home after he was questioned and his parents were called in. If his break-ins had been discovered, he wouldn't have gotten off so easily. The Motoki family had no idea about those. They probably couldn't even imagine such a thing.

Haruo's parents had already apologized to Sakura's parents many times, and they wanted this time to be the last. He worried that they were going to send him to family court if things went on like this. Because he'd been habitually truant and in trouble with the police, his parents had had conferences with both his homeroom teacher and the head of the school, and everyone agreed that it was time to do something. None of the adults objected to his dropping out of school and moving to Tokyo to work at the pastry shop. They in fact relentlessly tried to persuade him to do so. Under pressure from his parents, all he could do was shamelessly cry and beg, but when his brother Tsubasa threatened him with a metal bat, he relented. It was a solution that the Motoki family, for the time being at least, was also willing to accept.

●

He felt a light tapping on his right shoulder and opened his eyes. "We're here," the older woman told him, smiling. Haruo realized he had dozed off. The smile never leaving her face, the woman bowed to him as she had when they were leaving port, and slung her *zudabukuro*, a shoulder bag used by monks and pilgrims, across her shoulder. As she was leaving, he bowed slightly back to her, as unsociably as ever.

He stood up, slipped on his backpack, and couldn't help but look over at seat 15D. The girl was still asleep, even though most of the passengers had disembarked.

Following what the old woman had done for him, he approached her and touched her shoulder.

"Hmm... what? Huh?"

"We've arrived."

"Oh... thank you."

Rubbing her eyes with the back of her hands, she stood up briskly, as if she hadn't just been asleep a few seconds ago. Haruo turned around and made haste for the exit. He didn't want her to think he was trying to be alone with her, or that he had some ulterior motive; he also didn't want to fall into his bad habit of talking more than necessary. Today and tomorrow he would have to carry out his mission in exacting detail; he didn't have the luxury of wasted words or actions. He recalled that his talkativeness was the thing that "Sakura-chan" hated most about him, and so he made the effort to keep his mouth shut.

Haruo took the escalator down to the first floor of Ryotsu Terminal and stepped up to the car rental counter. He had made his reservation online, and as he now had to produce his driver's license, he couldn't give a false name or address. This meant that he couldn't leave a single drop of blood behind in the car.

He had rented the cheapest subcompact available— a silver Daihatsu Mira, with automatic transmission and power steering—not only because of price but because he'd learned online that the island's narrow roads weren't suited for larger cars. He was a novice driver anyway and wasn't planning to take the ibises as cargo with him, so a small car would do.

The rental agent took him to the lot and handed him the key. Haruo opened the door gingerly. He hadn't touched a steering wheel since he'd passed his driving test. In Tokyo, there were so many lanes and so much traffic that he was afraid to drive there. Now he regretted that he hadn't practiced at least a couple of times in the city. It was his first time driving alone too, and he felt self-conscious stepping on the accelerator as the agent stood alongside him watching.

He was tense and his palms were sweaty as he pulled out of the lot. At the intersection just beyond the lot, he waited for the signal and noticed the girl from the boat standing on the side of the road. She seemed to be in a predicament, her head drooping, her cell phone in one hand, as if her ride hadn't shown up. Their eyes met, and he raised his right hand.

She stepped up to the car. "Excuse me, are you from Sado?" she asked.

He was about to reply when the light changed and the driver behind him honked. Haruo felt flustered, uncertain how to react, and the driver behind started honking some more. "Hold on a minute," he said to the girl, and drove ahead. He took an immediate left, pulled over onto the shoulder a few meters from the intersection, and yanked the parking brake.

●

The time was 2:50 p.m. His plan had been to be at the forest park in Niibo Village surveying the Sado Island Crested Ibis Preservation Center at that moment. Instead, he was still only a short distance from Ryotsu Port, strolling around a shopping arcade in the harbor district. He was with the girl, and they were trying to decide where to eat. They had hardly introduced themselves when she asked, "Have you had lunch?" He was so delighted by this that he didn't mind veering from his schedule. Earlier they'd passed a house on the avenue with the sign "Ikki Kita's Birthplace." "Who's Ikki Kita?" they both muttered at the same time and looked at each other and laughed. Haruo felt completely at ease in such amiable company. Come to think of it, it was the first time in a long time that he'd actually had a conversation with someone.

Her name was Fumio Segawa, and she was an eighth-grader living in Tokyo. Over lunch she said that she would turn fourteen in six days, and that she absolutely had to visit Sado Island before that.

They went into a soba restaurant called Kogetsu. Since his parents ran a soba restaurant he was about to suggest going elsewhere, but Fumio piped up first: "Why don't we have some soba?" Haruo was willing to agree. As they parted the *noren* at the entrance, he told himself that, in this case, it was best to compromise and save time.

Punctuating her slurping with "It's so yummy!" she told him more about herself.

She'd been planning this, her first solo trip, for three months.

She'd kept it secret from her parents, telling them that she was staying at a friend's tonight. She'd saved up the money by working part-time at a sake store owned by a relative. Two months ago she'd met someone online who lived on Sado, and when she told him her plans to go there, he promised to be her guide on the island, and said she could stay at his place for the night. But when she arrived, the "email pal" who was supposed to pick her up at the terminal wasn't any-where to be found. With nowhere to turn, she was on the verge of tears when her savior showed up. That savior was Haruo.

When she bumped into him at the ticket gate in Niigata, she thought he seemed kind of scary, but when they arrived in Ryotsu and he tapped her on the shoulder to wake her up, she thought he was a nice person.

"I guess destiny brought us together," Fumio said. Haruo felt his heart race. He was about to say that they were on the same train too, but he didn't want her to think he'd been eyeing her all along.

He asked her if it wasn't too early to give up on her "email pal," since the jetfoil had arrived precisely on schedule at 2 p.m. Fumio pouted and shook her head. She showed him the message on her cell phone.

What? You actually came? For real? You're so stupid! Wait as long as you want, I'm not coming. I don't live on Sado. I don't even live in Niigata! LOL!! Don't trust people you meet online, little girl! Listen to your parents from now on. Good luck, and have a nice trip!

Not only had he not come to meet her, the store where he told her to wait didn't exist. Worried, she had quickly sent him an email, and that was his reply.

"That's horrible," Haruo said in a high, nasal voice,

tips of his chopsticks still in his mouth. She looked back at him with moist eyes. "Should I kill him for you?" he said.

Fumio nodded. "I'm really angry enough to want that. I'll never forgive him!"

Haruo had had a brush with email fraud himself. He'd almost been victimized by the guy who said he had a "Tokarev (8 rounds included)" he wanted to sell. When Haruo hesitated, the guy wrote, "Transfer the money right away!" Followed by: "Why aren't you replying? Send the money soon or you'll be sorry."

Pretty sure that this was a scam, Haruo wrote back "I'm sorry, I don't need it anymore."

"You chicken shit!" the guy replied. "You're just some stupid kid, I bet. If you're such a wimp, don't go posting that you want a real gun!"

Now this got Haruo pissed off, and he pounded this out: "Listen, you hopeless little dick-cheese punk, you lucked out. You don't seem to have any imagination, but since you're so worked up, here's a little bit about me, special just for you: I'm not the helpless and timid little kid you think I am. And I would never imitate some dipshit like you. I'm going to do something huge, and it's going to happen soon. In the fall, on a certain island. Trust me, it's going to rock your world. That's all for now. If I feel like it, I might tell you more later. If you behave yourself."

He'd lost his cool and wound up spilling part of his plan, but only to some stupid outlaw wannabe. And besides, the exchange took place over free email, which didn't reveal his personal information. He wasn't worried about having it traced back to him.

The conversation between Haruo and Fumio would have naturally turned at this point to their respective reasons for being there. Yet despite having moved in that direction, they suddenly started saying less and less. They each seemed to harbor something, but Haruo kept quiet and Fumio also seemed reluctant to get to the heart of the matter.

He looked at the clock: already past 3:30 p.m. He only had an hour to make it to the Crested Ibis Museum, but he couldn't just leave her here. She said she'd already bought her return ticket, but, perhaps because she'd put too much faith in her "email pal," she only had 3,000 yen on her. This aroused Haruo's protective tendencies. Even if he gave her some money, if he left her alone there was always the chance that someone else would take advantage of her. She was too yielding, and a little bit dense. Nonetheless, there was no way he could carry out his mission with Fumio Segawa in tow. She would only get in the way, and he didn't want her getting mixed up in everything. *What can I do?*

Seeing how Haruo lowered his eyes and seemed to be turning over thoughts in his mind, Fumio decided that she could come clean with Haruo. She too had a hidden agenda.

"You see, the truth is... I want to go to Sai no Kawara. Mr. Toya! Is there anything you have to do around there? Sai no Kawara is in the northern part of the island, near Onogame and Futatsugame... on the coast. Would you like to go there?"

Haruo paused. "Uh, yeah. Sure," he got around to saying. "I thought I'd take a look around there myself..."

What the hell are you saying?! he screamed in his mind. He had no idea what Sai no Kawara was, but he felt he had to help the poor young girl.

"I know it's a lot to ask, but could you take me there? Please? I have to go to Sai no Kawara, no matter what! I'm begging you!"

She bowed to him. Haruo's heart was ready to burst.

He told her he would only do it on three conditions: she had to stick to his schedule; she wouldn't ask him what he was doing; and she wouldn't tell anyone that they'd spent time together on Sado. All three of these made him seem suspect, but he had no choice.

Without a shadow of misgiving, Fumio nodded vigorously. "I won't make any demands. As long as I can go to Sai no Kawara, that's all that matters. That's all I care about. When that liar didn't show up, I was so worried I'd wasted everything coming here, but you came to my rescue! Thank you!" she said, bowing to him again.

"In that case," Haruo said, "how about going to see the crested ibises? They're only about ten minutes from here by car..."

●

At 3:55 p.m., they arrived at the Niibo Village Crested Ibis Forest Park. There were about a dozen cars and five tourist buses in the parking lot. A surprisingly large number of visitors were gathered in front of the shops outside the park. There hadn't been that many passengers on the jetfoil, but it seemed many people came to see the ibises on weekends. The visitors from the tourist buses were speaking Kansai dialect, and most of the license plates on the cars were from outside of Niigata Prefecture. A fair number seemed to have come by car ferry or airplane. This would make it harder to narrow down suspects, he thought. In any case, as long as he didn't leave any evidence behind, the investigation wouldn't get very far. This put him at ease a bit.

There was nothing of interest in the museum itself. He already knew almost all of the information presented there; in terms of his mission, the building wasn't particularly important.

Haruo purchased two admissions from the ticket machine, which was marked "Contributions for Environmental Conservation." They passed through the museum entrance and went straight to the ibis cage "observation zone."

The scene was no different from the ones he had seen in countless photographs taken from every angle, so many that he'd gotten sick of them. The cages were lined up side by side, surrounded by trees, with grass on the ground. There was a pond in the middle of the courtyard. And there in the cages, lo and behold, were the ibises. From this distance of around fifty meters they looked absurdly small, but there was no doubt that they were actually the ibises.

Haruo was left cold. He didn't feel an iota of emotion. Instead, his mind turned immediately to practical matters, comparing the actual terrain to what he had imagined in his planning. His senses grew sharp, his concentration keenly focused.

"Mr. Toya, look, those binoculars are free," Fumio called out.

Haruo wasn't happy about having his name spoken out loud in public. Fumio was so innocent, however, that he couldn't feel angry. He just clenched his teeth as he nodded, then began to survey every corner of the grounds with the binoculars.

Despite all his web searches, he hadn't been able to check on one part of the conservation center's security system until now: there were infrared sensors everywhere. Haruo pulled out his notebook and wrote down the positions of all the sensors he could see. The sensors were attached to posts that were knee- to waist-high, and there were at least ten of them on the grounds. It seemed almost impossible to make his way the fifty meters from the fence to the cages without being detected by one of them. But perhaps because the sensors were placed at fairly regular intervals, he might determine a route that weaved around them. He would compare his notes against the photo of the entire grounds that he had on his hard disk.

Next, with the binoculars he checked the door knob of the cage closest to the fence. One glance told him it was an integrated lock system. A smile came to his lips. An integrated lock with a keyhole in the center didn't even need to be picked; it could easily be wrenched open. The door itself had a glass window in the upper half, with no trace of any security measures. Haruo now felt sure that his mission would succeed.

But there were still obstacles to overcome. Surveillance cameras were constantly recording activity inside the cages. Cutting the cables one by one would not be easy. And then there was an infrared camera inside the cages whose feed was likely visible to the administrative offices at any time of the day or night. Even if he were recorded by that camera, Haruo reasoned, his identity would be obscured by the balaclava he'd be wearing. Same with the cameras recording ibis activity. His lingering worry was the high likelihood that the camera had a direct link to the security system. Supposing that was the case, he'd have to leave things to destiny. But in this, as in all else, Haruo had complete faith in his destiny.

Security at the Sado Island Crested Ibis Conservation Center was contracted out to Niigata Integrated Security, according to the sticker at the top of the doors to the cages. He would find the company's Sado-branch address online after he checked in to the hotel, then he'd time the drive from their office to the conservation center.

It was almost 5:00 p.m. His first scouting trip was almost done.

●

Haruo had chosen to stay at the Sado Grand Hotel on the shore of Lake Kamo. The reasons were simple: it was only five or six minutes from the Niibo Village Forest Park, and he was able to book online.

When he checked in, he changed the number of guests from one to two, telling the clerk that his sister—in the person of Fumio Segawa—would be staying with him. She had promised that she would repay the 15,000 yen added to his bill, but Haruo refused, saying that they would probably never meet again. He hadn't made a conscious decision never to see her again, but for some reason that's what he said.

Having now actually seen the conservation center, Haruo felt a transformation in his consciousness. He was neither passive and depressed, nor burning with excitement; rather, his senses had sharpened incredibly. It was a strange feeling—complete coolness and perfectly clear judgment. Was this the so-called state of equanimity? The change was certain yet somehow subtle, and Haruo himself didn't comprehend what it meant.

After dinner, while Fumio was at the hotel's public baths, he went over the details of his plans. He found the address of Niigata Integrated Security office in Sado—357/7 Nakahara Terahata, Sawata-machi—which, from the map, seemed not very far from the conservation center. The guards would know the route well, and with no traffic in the middle of the night, if the alarm was triggered, they could be on-site pretty quickly. According to the Niigata Integrated Security website, when an alarm is triggered, guards first rush to the scene of the break-in and then, if necessary, call the police. A confrontation thus seemed inevitable. Haruo needed to incapacitate the guards before they could contact the police. In twenty hours he would face that test.

"Mr. Toya, you're not going to take a bath?"

Fumio had tossed all reserve aside and was acting as if she and Haruo really were brother and sister. Haruo, deep in concentration, found her relaxed familiarity a bit irritating.

She had been very curious about him. He had nonchalantly suggested that they go see the ibises but, once at the center, he turned deadly serious, inspecting every aspect of the center meticulously and taking notes. Although she had promised not to ask him why he was on Sado, she was itching to bombard him with questions. Haruo was alert to that, and before she could say anything, he would distract her by cracking a joke or telling a story.

"I have to tell you something, Miss Segawa. I know this might be a surprise but, actually, I'm not Japanese."

"Huh? But... you look so Japanese..."

"I told you I'm from Yamagata, didn't I? Well, long ago, the regions north of Yamagata were not a part of Japan."

"North of Yamagata... You mean, the Tohoku region?"

"That's right. But I don't mean it's because it's in the middle of nowhere or something like that. On the border between Niigata and Yamagata prefectures, there's a mountain called Nihonkoku—"The Country of Japan." Have you heard of it? You haven't, have you? The name is kind of a joke. That mountain was the northern boundary of Japan in ancient times. That's why it's called "The Country of Japan." I found that out in a book."

"Really?"

"That's why I'm not Japanese. Isn't that interesting?"

This may have sounded like Haruo just making up a story out of whole cloth, but Haruo had indeed read this in a book. In fact, in his preoccupation with crested ibises, Haruo had bought several books about Sado, which he flipped through, zeroing in on what he thought were the most interesting bits. The story about Nihonkoku came from the *Encyclopedia of Mysterious Niigata*, edited by Moriaki Hanagasaki.

It seemed many historically significant temples and cultural artifacts were produced in the northern extremity of the former Echigo Province, which was itself at the border of ancient Japan and the lands known as Ezo. Since it was the frontier between the area controlled by the Yamato court and the area controlled by the Emishi people in Ezo, it came to be called "Nihonkoku."

His scattered reading actually turned up things that seemed to have direct bearing on himself too... From *An Illustrated History of Sado*, edited by Yoshiharu Honma, in a section on "The Crested Ibis in Japanese History: Place Names and Family Names," there was this:

Nagai City is located in the Dewa Hills on the right bank of the Mogami River in southwestern Yamagata Prefecture. During the Nanbokucho Period, it was a hamlet that bore the name Toya, as per the territorial allotment order of one Date Muneto, dated October 1380: Country of Dewa, Okitami County, Nagai Manor, Toya Hamlet. In the Muromachi Period the hamlet came to be known as Tokiniwa, written with the kanji for crested ibis. In the Edo Period the hamlet grew into a village.

This was an unexpected convergence of facts. Haruo was born in Yamagata, so of course it was reasonable to believe that the Toya family originated in Nagai City and not Chiba as he had earlier imagined. Important other considerations emerged.

From the same source:

The Crested Ibis is an internationally protected bird and special national protected species. During the rebuilding and rededication of the Ise Grand Shrine that occurs every twenty years, the Sugari no Ontachi sacred sword has two crested ibis feathers tied to its handle with a red silk thread. The tradition has continued for over a thousand years. These rare birds can also be found in China.

From "The Demise of the Sado Gold Mine: Closing the Book on 400 Years of History":

The Sado mine in Aikawa-machi closed on the last day of March 1989. The announcement had been made on January 7 of that year and took the people of Sado by surprise. The same day, television and radio stations broadcast the news that the Showa emperor had passed away in the Fukiage Palace, signaling the end of an era.

Thus, Haruo concluded, the crested ibis, the gold mine, and the emperor constituted the three points of a triangle—"the triangle of nobility." The Sado gold mine and the Showa emperor had already reached their end; only the crested ibis lived on, trying to breed and survive. *I will end you soon.*

After several detours, the time would finally come for him to carry out the final solution to the *Nipponia nippon* problem.

●

Haruo, to guarantee the success of his mission, needed more reconnaissance, this time at night.

The Yokojuku line was a narrow, unlit stretch that ran from National Highway 350 toward Niibo Village.

He drove it alone in the darkness, which was both exhilarating and nerve-racking. Even though he had grown up in a similar environment, the deserted country roads at night felt very eerie.

As he turned off the Yokojuku line onto the road leading to the Niibo Village Crested Ibis Forest Park, he took the precaution of slowing down and, at the gates to the park, turned his headlights off. He slowly entered the parking lot, where he saw only a single mini-truck. He'd seen it earlier that day and knew it was used for maintenance around the park.

Flashlight in hand, he slipped through a gap in the sliding gate in front of the museum, then found himself in the observation zone. The grounds of the conservation center were dark and silent. Scaling the fence would be easy. There was no sign of surveillance.

He made his way to the area in front of the main gate. It was brightly illuminated by a large panel light, which Haruo thought might be cause for worry. One car was parked in front of the administration building. Probably it was a night watchman's, but there seemed no additional sign of security. This would give him some time before anybody got in his way.

Having seen the conditions of the center at night, Haruo felt reassured that his plan would work.

Returning to the parking lot, he looked up at the sky. It was completely overcast: no stars and no moonlight. *Everything is exactly how I thought it would be.*

He returned to the hotel, took the elevator to the third floor, and quietly opened the door to his room. Only the nightlights were on, and Fumio Segawa seemed to be asleep in her futon on the tatami-mat floor.

He put down his backpack and took a bottle of orange juice out of the refrigerator. He looked out at the ink-black landscape. With the exception of the few minutes he'd dozed off on the jetfoil, he hadn't slept since the night before, but he wasn't sleepy at all.

"You're back."

Haruo started and almost spilled his orange juice. Fumio was staring up at him from her futon.

There was a long silence. The atmosphere between them had changed since lunch in the soba restaurant. They could both sense that, but there was a difference in how they understood the quality of the feeling. Fumio couldn't stand the strain any longer.

"Why did you come to Sado?" she asked.

Haruo didn't answer. He placed the bottle on the table, worried that it might crack in his grip. The back of his neck was burning.

"I mean, what —"

"That's enough. Just stop."

"But Mr. Toya…"

"No, no, just leave me alone."

Fumio pulled the comforter up to her eyes. But she didn't stay quiet. "I don't really know you that well… but… you seem like a good person to me. So…"

"Look, what are you trying to say? You aren't making any sense."

"I saw those things. I mean, I didn't mean to, I just wound up seeing them. Earlier. A few times. The things in your bag."

"Oh. I see."

"Mr. Toya, are they —"

"Stop, Sakura-chan, that's enough! I've finally found my mission in life. I have no doubts anymore. And tomorrow, I'm going to achieve it, no matter what. Stop trying to lead me astray! I'm begging you! You never said anything, you never explained, you just went and died! That was heartless! No matter how you look at it, that was just too cruel! Let me do what I want! You can't keep me tied down forever. There are things I need to do. If I can't do them, my life will be worthless!"

When Haruo was done, the only sound in the room was that of Fumio crying. Haruo closed his eyes and crouched down in a squat, trying to calm himself and catch his breath.

For several minutes neither of them spoke. Then, sniffling, Fumio said softly, "I'm sorry."

Haruo could not respond. He stayed in his crouched position while more time passed.

Slowly he stood up and walked to the door, ready to leave. Fumio leaped out of her futon. "Wait, where are you going?" she asked.

Haruo paused, then replied, "To take a bath."

Fumio started to apologize again.

"No, it's fine," Haruo said, stopping her. "I'm the one who should apologize. Something is screwed up in my head. I'm sorry." He turned, left the room, and shut the door.

Haruo did not go to the baths. He went to the parking lot, sat in the driver's seat of his rental car, and focused on what he would do the following night. He would do this until dawn, to wipe away any residue of hesitation.

●

They checked out of the hotel at 10 a.m. and set out for the village of Negai in Ryotsu City.

They didn't take the direct route along the Uchikaifu coast. Feeling bad that he had made Fumio cry the night before, Haruo decided to take a scenic route as a way to make up for it, to cheer her up. Heading in the direction of Kanai, they went up the Osado Skyline Road to the highest point on the island (elevation: 942 meters), where they stopped to look out at the view. Haruo didn't say anything, but Fumio smiled and seemed in good cheer. From there they drove along the Sotokaifu coast through Aikawa, stopping to look at the bare rocks and the sea, then continuing along a road that was barely wide enough for one car. Traveling along the edge of the island, they passed through Onogame and arrived at Sai no Kawara.

The waves were rough and the rocks were slippery, but Fumio Segawa walked toward the beach without hesitation. Haruo followed after her in silence. The further along the path they went, the taller the waves seemed, and the more their field of vision was filled with spray. They were soaking wet by the time they reached the cave, which had been turned into a shrine to the bodhisattva Jizo, the patron deity of dead and aborted children. Countless stone Jizo statues lined the cave.

From her orange bag, Fumio brought out a soft plastic Pikachu doll and placed it in front of the statues.

She placed her hands together in reverence, gently lowered her head, her eyes closed, and began to pray. The sea spray continued to batter them mercilessly, but Fumio didn't move an inch as she said her prayer for the dead.

As they headed back to Ryotsu Terminal, Fumio explained. The Pikachu had belonged to her little brother. He had been hit and killed by a train the past April, just as he was beginning elementary school. The accident was her fault.

"I got a letter from someone I hate. I threw it onto the tracks. He thought I dropped it by accident. He went to get it for me..."

She broke down in tears but kept going.

Since his death, her parents had been inconsolable. Their grief was unending. She was responsible for his death, and she couldn't bear the thought of facing her fourteenth birthday as if nothing had happened. She had heard about the cave at Sai no Kawara, and she resolved to have a memorial service for him there.

When she had finished, it was Haruo's turn: "Someone who meant a lot to me died this spring also."

Sakura Motoki, he said, jumped off the roof of her high school on April 29, ending her life. He didn't learn about it until he returned home for the driver training camp. No one had told him. When he found out, he stormed into the Motoki house and screamed at her father, "I warned you this would happen!" They pushed each other around, came to blows. He was almost arrested by the police.

What happened was that Sakura and her math teacher had started sleeping together over the winter break. When the new school year started in spring, the teacher was transferred to another school. Young Sakura felt abandoned and lost, and decided to kill herself.

In the days after he learned about this tragedy, Haruo fell into a state of collapse. He stopped his driving lessons. He spent time alone, in grief and at a loss about what to do. But as he pondered his destiny, he began to think that perhaps Sakura's death was also a part of it. That was the only way that he could bear the harsh reality. All he had left was his belief in that destiny. He had to focus on bringing it to pass.

Haruo parked the car along the road in front of the Ryotsu South Pier building, near where he and Fumio started this journey together. They got out of the car and walked to the escalator, where they faced each other to say their goodbyes. This would be the last time they spoke.

"Thank you so much," Fumio began. "You really saved me. I'm so glad I met you. Thank you, thank you! Mr. Toya... I... I don't know what to say..."

Haruo frowned and lightly patted her left shoulder. "Forget everything that happened," he said, and turned around to run back to the car. He thought he could hear Fumio calling out to him, but now he had only one thing on his mind.

●

At 11:23 p.m. on October 14, 2001, Haruo Toya initiated the "final solution to the Nipponia nippon problem." His destination: Cage A, situated in the innermost grounds of the Sado Island Crested Ibis Conservation Center. His target: Yu Yu, the male crested ibis sequestered there. His task: to kill Yu Yu.

Even at night, with empty roads, it takes twenty minutes to drive from the Niigata Integrated Security offices to the Niibo Village Crested Ibis Forest Park. Haruo had test-driven the route in his Mira at 10:00 p.m. He wouldn't have a lot of time to act. Earlier, he had bought two items: one was the largest scoop net available at a tackle shop near Ryotsu Port. The net would be used to capture Yu Yu; once Yu Yu was subdued, he would knife the bird to death. The other was a sewing kit from the convenience store along National Highway 350. The sewing kit contained a spool of red thread, which would be used to tie two of Yu Yu's feathers to the hilt of the knife used in the killing. And with that, the third point in the triangle of nobility would have been realized.

He climbed over the fence and slowly followed his predetermined route, using his flashlight sparingly. His footsteps on the grass seemed to grow louder with each step, which made him slow down and tread more cautiously. It took a full twenty minutes to reach the cage.

His stomach hurt he was so nervous, but he couldn't delay a second. He pulled the Trimo pipe wrench out of his backpack; holding the end of the flashlight with his teeth, he tightened the wrench around the door knob and began to turn it. Precisely at that moment, the flashlight went out. He shook it, thinking maybe the contact point was bad, but nothing happened. How could the battery be dead!

It was pitch black directly in front of him, but he wasn't shrouded in complete darkness. Light from

the large panel lamp on the main gate dimly illuminated the area here and there. There was no reason to
panic. What he needed to do was calm down and apply
enough torque to get the door to open. He took a deep
breath and with all his strength tried to get the knob
to turn. All that produced was the grinding sound of
metal against metal.

Frustrated, he was on the verge of despair.

He pulled off his balaclava, which had made him
feel hot and stuffy and more agitated. He rummaged
around in his backpack for his sports towel. He folded
it into quarters, placed it against the window, and
shattered the window with the pipe wrench. Shards
of glass fell to his feet. Paying no mind to the noise,
he reached in and twisted the thumb turn to open the
door. At last he was inside the cage. The fourth finger
on his left hand was bleeding, cut by the glass, but he
ignored the pain and blood. He also hadn't noticed
the alarm sensor installed in the frame of the window.

In the darkness Haruo could hear a bird squawking.
He shuffled forward, panting, his fist clenching the
handle of the scoop net. Then bird cries came from two
directions. He twisted around; there was the fluttering
of wings. A feather drifted down and stuck to his cheek,
which was drenched with sweat.

His eyes were slowly adjusting to the darkness, but he still could not track the birds' movements. Haruo was panting and wheezing, and he worried that this stalemate would not end. *I can't let this drag out,* he muttered to himself, *I have to hurry.* A bright light suddenly blinded him, and he turned away quickly. "What the hell are you doing!" someone yelled at him. His flagging concentration was suddenly laser-sharp again.

He shielded his eyes with his right arm and took a few steps back. The night guard rushed toward him and yelled, "You crazy son-of-a-bitch, what the hell are you doing here!" He tried to grab Haruo's raised arm, but Haruo leaned backwards and evaded his grasp. At that moment, the agility he had cultivated attacking people in the streets paid off. As the guard stumbled forward, Haruo pulled out the stun baton tucked in his belt and thrust to in the guard's chest. Without a moment's pause, he fired the gun.

For what felt like twenty or thirty seconds, a tiny lightning bolt flashed in the darkened cage. The guard let out a clipped groan, and fell to the ground.

●

It was a few minutes past midnight when the alarm sounded at the Niigata Integrated Security offices. The sensors on the conservation center's grounds were often triggered by stray cats and other animals, so the officer on duty, Kengo Oya, called the center to check on the situation. When the night guard didn't answer, Oya grew concerned. The phone at the center never rang more than ten times. This time, nobody picked up even after twenty rings. After forty rings without an answer, Oya hung up and grabbed the keys to his car.

At 12:35 a.m., he pulled up in front of the main gate.

He opened the door to the administration building. The lights of an inner room were on, but nobody was there. He called out. Silence. But there seemed to be some wild commotion coming from the cages. He could hear the terrible cries of the ibises. He went to the back of the administration building and entered the grounds, pointing his flashlight toward Cage A, where he could hear wild flapping and squawking.

From a distance he could see some large, unrecognizable dark body making jerking movements inside the cage. He rushed to the door, saw that it was open, and peered inside. He couldn't believe his eyes.

Somebody dressed in black was diving after the ibises waving a fishing net around. Dumbfounded, he took a couple of steps forward when his left foot stumbled over something, terrifying him. He pointed his flashlight down and was shocked to see the guard lying motionless on the ground. He began to grasp how bad the situation was. His training kicked in, and he turned his attention the intruder in black.

"Hey, you! Stop!" he yelled.

A stun baton was suddenly thrust in his face, and he recoiled. He was totally unprepared for that, and he froze as he heard the crackling of the weapon. Then it happened again and again. The intruder kept flicking the switch, and began to panic when it became clear the gun had lost its charge. Seeing this, Oya grabbed the intruder by his neck and tried to wrestle him down to the ground. Perhaps because he was too confident in his strength, perhaps because he didn't expect the unexpected, Oya had made himself vulnerable.

In an instant, his vision clouded over and his breathing grew labored. He writhed on the ground, realizing he'd been pepper sprayed. He also did not expect what came next: something sharp plunged right into his belly. He felt searing pain. He rubbed his eyes with his left arm, while his right hand reached toward his abdomen. He was bleeding out. He had been stabbed. He thought to call the police, but he could no longer stand and strength was draining from his body.

●

The security guard had barely managed to pull out his cell phone when he stopped moving. He was a silhouette sprawled out on the ground. The knife sticking out of him looked like an erect penis.

Spent, Haruo sank to the ground. The pepper spray was hanging in the air; the smell was unbearable and it was hard to breathe. He had been incapacitated by his own weapon. He didn't have all day to catch Yu Yu and Mei Mei, and he had had enough. *It doesn't matter anymore*, he thought, and threw the net against an iron pole.

He stayed sprawled on the ground, covered his face with both hands, and looked down. It felt as if time had stopped. His mind went back to yesterday, the day before, a week ago, a month ago, a year ago, then folded back into the present. He finally saw the truth, a hint of what had haunted him since the night before: destiny was meaningless. Completely meaningless.

He heard squawking outside the cage, and looked out onto the grounds. At some point, Yu Yu and Mei Mei had got out of their cage, and were now about to fly off into the night sky. Here was another unexpected scene. Haruo, even more exhausted, could only think: *OK, follow your desire. Test your luck. If it's bad, you know the way back. If it's good, fly wherever your heart takes you...*

●

With nowhere to go, Haruo parked in front of the Ryotsu South Pier building, the same spot where he had let Fumio off to live her life. He sat slumped in the driver's seat, his overalls spattered in blood. As lifeless as he might have felt, his emotions were a storm within him. He felt completely alone and filled with dread. To distract himself, he turned on the radio, where a pop song in English that he had never heard before was playing. The lyrics, especially the part about "I'm just a poor boy, I need no sympathy...," seemed custom-made for him.

The car's windows suddenly shattered and the doors flew open on both sides. A group of uniformed men stormed the car like an avalanche. They stuffed a rag in his mouth and yanked him out by his arms and legs.

As he was pulled to a waiting van, he saw several police cars parked there. The Ryotsu Police Station, it seemed, was right at the corner of the intersection.

●

As usual, Haruo woke up past noon, went to the kitchen, grabbed his bento lunch from the table, and went into the living room to watch TV. Nobody else was home.

His bento today had an omelet and macaroni salad. He liked omelets but hated macaroni salad. In the fourth grade, he had thrown up after eating some macaroni salad, and he'd hated it ever since. He'd also hated mayonnaise since that day, and wouldn't touch any for a full year afterwards. He dumped the macaroni salad in an ashtray, cursed his mother, and started inhaling the omelet.

On TV people were all in a flap about some kind of national outrage. A daytime talk show kept going on about how, on Sado Island, a security guard had been killed and two crested ibises, the endangered sacred bird of Japan, had escaped. This caught Haruo's interest, so he went up to his room, turned on his computer, and went online.

As expected, The Inside Dope forum was already on the story. This was always the case right after a big breaking event. Haruo quickly posted: "Another teenage suspect?" and followed it up with: "He killed someone, so he'll probably get five to six years, right?"

This got a response from someone that read: "Did he post anything online before doing it?"

This reminded Haruo about an ominous email exchange he'd had a while ago. Some person, probably a punk teenager, had been "looking for a real gun," and Haruo decided to fake a reply about having a "Tokarev (8 rounds included)" to sell. This teenager got irritated at some point and wrote in a fit that he was going to "do something huge."

Haruo went and checked his archived inbox, and when he located the email exchange in question, he couldn't contain his excitement. "In the fall, on a certain island" was clearly talk about what happened on Sado. Haruo had to brag about this so he posted the entire email exchange to The Inside Dope, claiming this was the kid who committed the crime.

Nobody believed Haruo. "Stop making up sloppy bullshit, kid," people told him. Thoroughly humiliated, Haruo insisted the story was true and gave a detailed chronology of what had happened. It wasn't enough. People said he needed more objective proof.

Haruo thought hard about how to get people to believe him, but he couldn't think of how to prove that the email exchange was real. Being ganged up on and treated like a dumb kid had made him furious. He had to clear his head.

He looked out the window and thought he should get out of the house and allow the waves of emotion to subside. Maybe that wouldn't be such a bad idea. He hadn't been out in forever.

MORE FROM PUSHKIN'S
JAPANESE NOVELLA SERIES

KAORI FUJINO

NAILS AND EYES

KAZUSHIGE ABE

NIPPONIA NIPPON

NATSUKO IMAMURA
AUTHOR OF THE WOMAN IN THE PURPLE SKIRT

**THIS IS AMIKO,
DO YOU COPY?**

NISHIOKA KYŌDAI

KAFKA

TOH ENJOE

**HARLEQUIN
BUTTERFLY**

KUMI KIMURA

**SOMEONE
TO WATCH
OVER YOU**

JAPANESE FICTION
AVAILABLE AND COMING SOON
FROM PUSHKIN PRESS

MS ICE SANDWICH
Mieko Kawakami

MURDER IN THE AGE OF ENLIGHTENMENT
Ryūnosuke Akutagawa

THE HONJIN MURDERS
Seishi Yokomizo

RECORD OF A NIGHT TOO BRIEF
Hiromi Kawakami

SPRING GARDEN
Tomoka Shibasaki

COIN LOCKER BABIES
Ryu Murakami

THE DECAGON HOUSE MURDERS
Yukito Ayatsuji

SLOW BOAT
Hideo Furukawa

THE HUNTING GUN
Yasushi Inoue

SALAD ANNIVERSARY
Machi Tawara

THE CAKE TREE IN THE RUINS
Akiyuki Nosaka